FUGU

A TALE OF ONE OF US

OTHER TITLES IN THE SERIES

FUGUE

A TALE OF ONE OF US

Milutin Cihlar Nehajev

Translated by
Damir Janigro

CEU PRESS

Central European University Press

Budapest–Vienna–New York

Published in 2023 by

Central European University Press

Nádor utca 9, H-1051 Budapest, Hungary
Tel: +36-1-327-3138 or 327-3000
E-mail: ceupress@press.ceu.edu
Website: www.ceupress.com

Edited by Ellen Elias-Bursać
Originally published in Croatian as *Bijeg,* 1909

ISBN 978-963-386-722-8
ISSN 1418-0162

A catalogue record for this book is available from the Library of Congress.

Contents

Translator's Preface

In memory of my mother Neda Cihlar,
and uncle Zvonimir "Sinek" Cihlar
and for my uncle Milutin 'Žuga' Cihlar

My father, Antonio Janigro, was a celebrated cellist and conductor renowned for founding the Zagreb Soloists in 1954. Despite being born in Italy in 1918, he chose to reside in Croatia during World War II to evade conscription into Mussolini's army for the ill-fated war in Russia. While he achieved international acclaim, his musical career remained centered in Zagreb. In tribute to his lasting impact, the city of Zagreb regularly hosts the Antonio Janigro Cello Competition. I had the opportunity to attend the most recent competition in January–February 2020, a time when the COVID-19 pandemic was beginning to emerge, and shortly before a devastating earthquake struck Croatia's capital city. As I searched for a friend at the music institute, a young man approached me and remarked: "Although I never had the privilege of meeting your father, he was an extraordinary man. Nevertheless, I find it surprising that you and your family haven't given the recognition that your Croatian grandfather, Milutin Cihlar Nehajev, deserves. He is well-known in our country but remains relatively unknown abroad." I readily agreed with his observation but continued the search for my friend.

As I embarked on the never-ending journey back to Cleveland, a sense of shame washed over me for never having delved into the literary works of Nehajev, a man revered as a remarkable writer, opera and classical music critic, and intellectual figure of the early twentieth century. Despite his illustrious reputation, he had passed away years before my birth, leaving me with only fragmented details shared by my mother. A solitary portrait of him adorned the walls of my parents' house, constantly reminding me of my limited knowledge of his opus. Driven by a determination to amend this gap in my understanding, I resolved to immerse myself in his writings. Without hesitation, I placed an order on Amazon for his book, originally titled *Bijeg* but later translated to *Fugue* by myself.

After reading *Fugue*, I was disheartened to discover that only a Croatian version existed, prompting me to undertake the translation of this exceptional literary work into English. However, the complexity of the Croatian language presented a significant challenge. Nehajev's writing style was angular and convoluted, requiring me to navigate intricate sentence structures and idiosyncratic punctuation. Nevertheless, I endeavored to capture the essence of his century-old style in modern English, and the results now lie before you for your judgment.

A personal reflection on *Fugue* is also warranted. Studying the novel not only allowed me to grasp its autobiographical aspects but also made me aware of a transgenerational connection. In many ways, Andrijašević, the protagonist, serves as Nehajev's alter ego. Both experienced academic difficulties and displayed remarkable literary ambitions and achievements from a young age. I also identified fragments of my own neuroses within Đuro's psychology. I have an aversion to travel and perceive it as an irreversible process of loss; I tend to lead a routine-based life and, like many others, sought solace in alcohol during challenging times. Nehajev briefly deviated from his life as an author and advocate of liberal arts; he earned a degree in chemistry and worked as a scientist. Similarly, I made a living as a scientist, but my true refuge has always been the amalgamation of "serious" music and literature.

Readers will draw their conclusions regarding the role of fate, self-destructive tendencies, depression, and alcoholism in Andrijašević's tragic life. Some may attribute his failure to the perpetual financial struggles of intellectuals who refuse to "sell their soul." Đuro himself offers explanations for his failures to his friend Toša. While translating this novel, I stumbled upon a sentence in Herman Melville's Pierre:

"He is learning how to live by rehearsing the part of death."

In my opinion, this is the best, yet involuntary, succinct summary of Đuro's life.

When translating *Bijeg*, I had two primary options in modern English: Escape or Fugue. While these words carry slightly different meanings, they were the obvious choices for rendering the word "bijeg." Although both imply running away from something, I favored the term "fugue" due to its musical connotations. While I cannot say for sure which option Nehajev would have chosen, "fugue" seems to best emphasize the lyrical aspects of the book. Considering Nehajev's passion for music, I also believed that "fugue" would do justice to his wide intellectual range. Both words convey the notion of fleeing from danger or something unpleasant, be it Đuro's escape from the city to the village or his reliance on alcohol to evade his demons. Ultimately, we are left uncertain about the true intent.

The novel *Fugue* is considered one of the most exceptional works of modern Croatian literature. It was published in 1909 and carried the subtitle *Povijest jednog našeg čovjeka* (The Story of One of Us). "Us" seems to refer to intellectuals or, in general, educated people who struggle to make a living. The book narrates the life and fate of Đuro Andrijašević, a destitute Croatian intellectual who receives an education in a major city but ultimately succumbs to the hardships of provincial life, leading to his ultimate downfall. Most of the content is autobiographical. Although the novel does not shy away from the economic and social aspects of life, the author primarily delves into the protagonist's state of mind, making it a psychological novel. And as a psychological novel, *Fugue* never ceases to surprise; the description of the protagonist's character takes center stage in the plot where mood changes, moments of crisis, or elation are masterly described. I rarely felt so close to a protagonist as I did to Andrijašević.

In *Fugue*, we can observe many features of modern prose. The author emphasizes internal characterization, conflicts, and frequent monologues by the main character through his letters and journals. *Fugue* comprises twelve chapters of varying lengths. The first chapter explores Đuro's thoughts during a nocturnal train journey, tracing his life from birth and childhood to completing his studies. This is masterfully done, and in a few pages we learn about the inner workings of Đuro's psyche. The subsequent chapters cover the following two years of his life, with the plot unfolding at a slow pace, focusing more on the internal musings of the main character than on the events surrounding him.

Milutin Cihlar Nehajev was a renowned Croatian journalist, playwright, writer, and storyteller. Born on November 25, 1880, in Senj to his parents Milica and Sebald, who worked in the trade chamber in Senj, he had Czech roots through his father. The word *cihlar* translates to "bricklayer". Milutin earned great esteem as an essayist and literary critic due to the numerous works he penned. He held a deep emotional attachment to the village of Senj in Dalmatia and frequently incorporated it into his literary creations. In fact, he adopted the pseudonym Nehajev himself, derived from the Nehaj Fortress in Senj. Cihlar attended high school in Zagreb and Vienna and later pursued studies in chemistry in Vienna. However, his true passion lay in literature, and he never pursued a career in science. In 1903, he earned his doctorate in philosophy in Vienna and, a year later, began working as a teacher at a gymnasium in Zadar. While in Zadar, he edited the well-known magazine "Lovor."

Nehajev entered the world of literature in the late nineteenth century, a period marked by ongoing disputes between different factions of older and younger generations. He laid the foundation for his literary career at a young age when his play *Prijelom* (Fracture) was published in 1897, followed by another play, *Svjećica* (Thin candle), just a year later. He diligently worked to establish his reputation, and his literary critiques continue to be highly regarded today. Alongside his literary output, he pursued a career as a journalist, editor, and publicist. While Milutin Cihlar initially focused on short stories and plays, which contributed to his recognition as a prominent modernist, he also made noteworthy contributions to theater and the visual arts through his extensive knowledge in these fields.

The Vienna phase of his creative journey held great significance in shaping his literary direction but, on the other hand, had a somewhat destructive impact on his spirit, leading to increasing bouts of depression. This is chronicled in Đuro's life in the metropolis. He drew inspiration from literature, finding influence in the works of Flaubert, Zola, and Ibsen. Throughout his writing, he aimed to capture art, often depicting fragments of himself within his characters. This was evident in his work *Studija o Hamletu* (A study of Hamlet), written in 1915, where he delved into Hamlet's character and his own internal world.

Initially, Milutin pursued innovative political ideals, but his stance changed when he joined the newspaper *Jutarnji List* in 1912, aligning himself with official politics. As a result, he often faced criticism from his admirers.

Milutin Cihlar Nehajev's body of work can be divided into several periods. The first phase, or his early phase, was influenced by pre-modernism, with his prose heavily drawing from realism. However, he gradually distanced himself from realism and began to explore more spiritual analysis.

His work's most significant phase is the one leading up to World War I, during which he fully immersed himself in modernism. It was during this time that he published the novel *Bijeg* (Fugue) and the collection *Veliki Grad* (The big city).

In the third phase, between the two world wars, Milutin turned to depicting characters from real-life surroundings. Works from this period include *Kostrenka, Jubilej* (Anniversary), and *Onaj žutokosi* (That yellow-haired one).

Damir Janigro, Ph.D.
Cleveland Heights, OH
June 2023

"He is learning how to live by rehearsing the part of death"

Herman Melville, *Pierre or, The Ambiguities*

Chapter I

A rainy, dark day had sunk the metropolis in a translucent mist. The looming monotone facades of the buildings heightened the impression of a dead weight settling on people and things.

"And I have to travel on a day like this," thought Đuro Andrijašević, boarding the streetcar with a small valise. Through the wet windows of the car, one could see the street leading to the southern railway station from an even more dismal viewpoint. The dankness of the late autumn day infiltrated the bones and was reflected on the faces of his traveling companions who, shivering from the chill, had completely forgotten their usual Viennese prattle.

Since his youth, Andrijašević had developed a strong distaste for travel. In general, he'd embraced an uneventful life and readily endorsed the students' venerable tradition of spending whole days in a coffee shop and then walking the short distance between the University buildings and the usual tavern. He'd laughingly admit that he had visited the main streets of this imperial city only after three months in Vienna.

Yet his indolence alone could not explain why he was so affected by travel. Packing clothes, laundry, and books and having a rough trip in third-class cars are all annoying, but what's worse, Andrijašević panicked at every departure. The most bizarre thoughts about the journey's vast and queasy uncertainty, a sense of home-lessness, and a constant restlessness came to his mind. He remembered well the last trip from Zagreb when the Hrabars escorted him to the station on his way to Vi-enna; he was rude and hostile to everyone, including his fiancée. He tried and failed to hide his uneasiness. At the train station café, when everything seemed fine and he was just waiting for the train to leave, he became so nervous that Vera later mentioned this in a letter. Đuro replied but struggled to explain 'that unhappy feeling' and failed to find the right words to describe it even to himself. "I feel as if a terrible secret lurks behind every departure; as if we forfeit the bit of life we leave behind, this slice of life we shall never have back. And fear takes hold—as if I were in that new world hurrying to find something unfamiliar and new to which I will never grow accustomed. Perhaps all this is a consequence of childhood impressions; I rarely saw my father, not for more than a day or two at a time, and these encounters normally ended with us all close to tears. Father was al-ready accustomed to his frequent departures as required by his being a ship captain. But, these images of tearful goodbyes remain engrained in my soul." The excuses for his behavior, which he wrote in the letter, were gladly received by Vera and reassured her. Mrs. Hrabar, how-ever, refused to accept Andrijašević's explanations for a long time afterward, and the following winter, she vigorously insisted on Vera attending *debutante* dances, which did not seem right to the girl, even though the engagement had not yet been made public.

"I have always been against these student love affairs. But if you succumb to one, you still mustn't get overly involved."

When Andrijašević was informed that Vera would be attending 'only three' dances this year, he didn't know that Mrs. Hrabar's decision was the consequence of the recent farewell with Vera in Zagreb. He replied to Vera's letter after three weeks, apologizing rather coldly that he "did not wish to disturb her," which persuaded Vera's mother even more that this was a doomed 'student romance' and confirmed to her that Vera would have many tears left for Lent.

Today's departure seemed even more difficult than usual. He could barely stop himself from getting off the streetcar. Imprisoned in the narrow space, with many passengers pushing to grab hold of the leather strap used to steady oneself, he was suddenly swept by distress, imagining that all the folks around him were alien creatures sent there just to bother him. He felt compelled to get off at a stop, shivering from the cold and almost desperately savoring his pain; he waited for the conductor to strike the bell before boarding the tram again. Every sound seemed to pierce his brain, and he barely overcame this by noticing the irony of counting the blows to the bell.

He regained his composure only when the train left behind the first of the countless stations on the Viennese periphery. In the comfortable but overheated compartment, his mood brightened; shortly, he fell into a half sleep, still aware—above all other sounds—of the wheels' rhythmic clatter. The loud noise mingled with the remembrance of his last night in Vienna, the goodbyes to his friends, the memory of countless toasts, and the final pilgrimage to all the nightclubs they usually frequented. Once these memories had morphed into the foggy state generally followed by sleep, he felt on his shoulder the hand of the conductor, who was asking for his ticket.

It occurred to Andrijašević that he had not told the Hrabars about his travel plans. "Ah, so what? I'll write a postcard from Pest"—he remained calm and settled, as best he could, in the corner, covering his eyes with his hat.

*

When he awoke, it was almost completely dark. In the dimly flickering gaslight, Andrijašević noticed new faces. Two young men stood across from him in the compartment, speaking in Croatian. Andrijašević soon discovered they were also students returning home to southern Hungary. Although he was not inclined to make casual train acquaintances, he thought it made sense to spend the two hours waiting for the next train in their company. As soon as the conversation started (about politics, of course, of which Andrijašević was reluctant to talk but which interested the young men), the train arrived at Central Station. The hours passed quickly, and Andrijašević was pleasantly surprised that one of his two companions was familiar with his literary work. The only annoyance was that he had to answer queries about literary events and participate in a conversation about 'cultural compromises.' The young men proved to be powerful idealists; nonetheless, when both men departed three hours before Pest, Andrijašević was sorry to be left alone. He had a full twelve hours of travel ahead and knew very well that he would not be able to sleep most of that time.

Sleep did not return to his eyes. Lately, he had been coming home at dawn from the many doctoral exam celebrations. Though he was tired, he couldn't sleep, accustomed to staying up all night. He was also worried by the thought that he hadn't sent a postcard to Zagreb from Pest. "After all, I have to let them know ... And if they're waiting for me? ... After I received my doctorate, they surely thought I'd be coming to see them first ..."

Little by little, Andrijašević began to allow the intrusion of thoughts he'd kept at bay. During the final days in Vienna, he had not wanted to think about 'it'; now, 'it' was coming straight at him. He knew something must be done; he needed to fix 'it.' He was aware he was not being considerate if he visited a friend in Slavonia instead of going to Zagreb, where they expected him to propose officially to Vera as a newly minted doctor.

He lit a cigarette, stood up, and tried to look outside. But the darkness was too dense to see the houses along the railroad tracks. Only occasionally, after long intervals, would a bright spot appear.

"Black is this trip," thought Andrijašević and sat down again on the bench, staring at the wick of the gaslight.

... "It's odd that of all people, I am the one alone in this car. If anyone else were here, we could talk.... I wouldn't have to think. Eventually, sooner or later ... In any case— it's not kind of me; but what can I do? Go to her and tell her that nothing has yet been accomplished? ..."

"Foolish tribulations after all. How many people find themselves in far worse circumstances—and yet they don't think about killing themselves with worries. And my situation cannot be otherwise, so there you have it: I'll convince myself that all will be right soon."

"It's true, I am running away from them. This is how they will interpret my trip to Slavonia. The old lady in particular. She'll be right."

"But this is better. Had I arrived in Zagreb, I would have visited them as usual. Everyone would congratulate me, and then the old mother would suggest we go for a walk, or she'd come up with another way to be alone with me for a while. She would immediately bring up the engagement; this would not have been the end of the world. I do not think Vera ..." (Andrijašević shuddered; he was afraid to finish: I do not intend to *leave* Vera), "I know what I owe her; but the old hag would come again with the same question she had when Vera first confessed our love: 'How will you make a living?' And I would have to say that I was not planning an abrupt end to my research, and would have passed the professor's habilitation exam immediately had poor Uncle Toma not died. 'A professor's salary, my dear, is a pittance,' the old lady would say, and she would be right. And now? Uncle Toma died and left a mortgaged house when we all thought he'd be leaving a fortune ..."

"It's frightening to be so dependent. The English certainly do not count on inheritances. Nonsense! Why in the world did the English come to mind! Still, this is a real shame: I based my entire future life on a fortune that never materialized."

"What did the old man use his money for? He must have spent half of it gambling. Or maybe not; perhaps he was never wealthy. In Primorje, along the Adriatic coast north of Dalmatia, people who earn a pension of fifty forints plus twenty in an annuity are considered rich. And on top of this, he was a loner. Yet not even two thousand is coming to me. The blessed man sent me forty forints a month while he was alive."

"It's dreadful that one never knows how much we own in our families. A father tells nothing to the son about his business. (I am suddenly acutely mindful of business). If the late Uncle Toma had at least told me ... Never mind, it would have come too late anyway..."

"I still should have written to them before I left Vienna. Not writing was discourteous. Hell, as if I could have stayed away from the busy nightlife! Today an oral exam, tomorrow a party, the day after tomorrow with a group of friends, and so on; never a moment of peace to think wisely."

... "So what should I think? My misery will not be changing anyway. It is, in fact, just as well that I'm not going to Zagreb. In any case, the old lady doesn't like me; she might happen to give me a break. She has expected me to come for Vera; she might even have welcomed me with hostility. Everything can be better explained in a letter. Both she and Vera will see that my way is the best for the time being—and they will simmer down while I take the exam. Vera will argue with her mother to defend my reasons; if I were to speak to the old lady now, I might argue with her too. Yes, it is better that I go to Zdenci. Still, I must write to them from Slavonski Brod."

Andrijašević had the habit of expressing his thoughts by speaking out loud; so, even now, he ended the conversation with himself almost audibly. And telling himself that everything would be well and that he'd send them a postcard, he dropped his cigarette and closed his eyes. But he was well aware that his thoughts to embellish his situation were nothing more than inadvertent excuses meant to fool him. From the bottom of his soul, something was telling him: this is not a solution, you are just postponing the inevitable and you know Vera's happiness depends on what happens next. He voiced this aloud to bury the unpleasant thought: I cannot do otherwise!

And when he could not find peace, he lit another cigarette (the compartment was already full of smoke) and began to recite to himself as if he were acting for an unknown listener in his defense.

"The matter is quite simple. Student Đuka Andrijašević is in his third year of university, and he and Miss Vera Hrabar meet and fall in love. The young lady is twenty-one, the student—twenty-one and a half. Love, admission to her mother. Permission to correspond. Otherwise, everything must be kept secret."

"How are you going to support yourselves?" "I have an uncle who will leave me something." Đuro is still young; what does he care about the monthly income necessary for marriage! "And my literary work brings in a bit" (God, how I really believed in this stuff!) So all together: the regular salary and the remaining income should be around one hundred and fifty forints. "Do you really believe that?" Đuro told his future mother-in-law that he was certain; but she remained skeptical. Vera is courageous, so there was nothing else to do but allow correspondence."

"That was four years ago. (Argh! It has been four years—Andrijašević shuddered amidst his recollections). Đuro was a little late taking his exams and was enrolled in a doctorate just to be granted a title and find work, as he could no longer receive scholarships. Uncle Toma died. Died and left approximately two thousand to Đuro's mother, his sister, and nothing to the man's nephew.

"One must make an effort and take the exams; then everything will be well again. (*Then* it will be two years, maybe three—true; it is safe to presume). After that, I will have a salary of at least one hundred forints, so wasting time now worrying doesn't help."

"What if the old lady says this will take too long?"

Andrijašević is shocked at this thought; for the first time, he understands he has another way out: the Hrabars might rescind the commitment and marry Vera to someone else.

*

This new thought was hard to keep at bay. The next day, before noon (the time he was due to arrive in Brod, two o'clock, wasn't getting any closer), while the train roamed the endless plains, interrupted for brief moments by forests that were dark green, almost black, from the thick rain and a leaden sky, also almost black, Đuro watched the desolate and gloomy environment and became increasingly sad. "I'm no longer young, and that's why this unsettles me. It was a crazy idea to squander twenty-four hours by going to Brod. And the craziest thing is that no end is in sight; these endless, boundless steppes slow down my mind. In any case, my position in the world is hardly the most attractive."

The passengers were changing, coming and going, but Andrijašević was happy encountering no one. He sank into melancholy and started doubting he would ever reach his destination. The journey appeared to have no end—and he suddenly began to like that idea. Rapid and disjointed thoughts surfaced about traveling to Siberia, about a philosopher who always walked along railroad tracks, and about two or three secondary school professors, trapped in provincial life, suffering from persistent worries and having no hopes. He had read something like this somewhere in Turgenev: "Young men would sit together, drink tea and eat stale buns; how often the conversation focused on ideals, the future!—and yet these pathetic fellows do not suspect that many of them will waste their lives playing a card game on a Preference board or trying to adjust to a simple, suburban existence."

"I should do a little more thinking about what awaits me. I have never made a proper inventory of my life. All is well—and that's that! as the late Toma would say. But, wait, it all started to go poorly. Poorly? Not truly terribly, just in an unusual way. If only we'd arrive in Slavonski Brod! Toša is a cheerful philosopher; he will immediately apply his method to all these problems. The truth is life cannot be arranged into methodic formulas. And my position is now straightforward; I spent hours torturing myself without success, trying to decide my next move."

"Of course, letting time go by would be best. If this were only about me, I'd find the going easier; but as it is..."

Andrijašević recalls people whose lives are intermingled with his. Pictures begin to surface and become more real; and his whole past sweeps through his soul faster than the windows and houses disappear from view.

*

... Captain Bartol Andrijašević had a son who was born when—after twenty-five years of wandering across the seven seas—he finally came home to settle down. With the help of a senior official on the city council of Rijeka, he obtained the position of harbormaster in Kraljevica near Rijeka. He ended his days there, performing his job rather clumsily and pushing his son to write about lighthouses and barges as soon as the boy reached elementary school. Otherwise, Đuro remembered him only vaguely; a tall man with a hard face, wide-eyed laughter, and huge teeth, an image that didn't form easily in the boy's brain; his father died when he was just eight. After his father's death, Mother never progressed past grieving; she moved to Rijeka and there she sublet rooms to students. Đuro had been encouraged from his first school days to study science. No one doubted that something extraordinary would come of the boy. By the age of five, Đuro already understood better and knew more than the older students who had already finished elementary school. According to his secondary school teachers' statements, he was generally seen as an *enfant prodige*; at the time, there was no comparable talent in the school. This belief increased when some of Đuro's stabs at writing began to appear in youth magazines; at the age of seventeen, he was already an exceptional scholar in the eyes of fellow students and teachers.

His mother was convinced more than anyone. The daughter of a well-to-do family of merchants, she was raised at a preparatory school in Trieste and had a higher level of education than an ordinary city-dwelling woman would ever need. Hardships had erased much of her luster, but she maintained a deep understanding of most things as far as they had to do with her son. When she was left with him (two older sisters, married in Primorje, died the same year), her feelings for Đuro and concerns about his progress increased. As far as she could, she supported her son, bought him books, and paid for piano lessons; his uncle Toma, who didn't have a family, helped, and loved Đuro as if the boy were his own child. Uncle Toma called him Đuro, which is not a common name in Primorje (because Toma, a timber trader in Lika, absolutely wanted the baby to be baptized with that name and was angry when Bartol yelled the name 'Jura'). The family had already assumed that an adored husband would emerge from this otherwise physically frail boy. This was supported by Aunt Klara, who—remembering that on her mother's side the whole family consisted of brilliant people, often living adventurously—said emphatically: "This boy will become either somebody or nobody."

Đuro's life in lyceum passed without major upheavals; at the age of eight, he was given access to an entire library. Before his graduation, his first major work came out in *Vijenac*; everyone marveled at this beginner's formal perfection. It was only through intense study and the constant reading of any and all books that this young, knowledgeable, eager soul had digested it all. No wonder with such efforts, the young man's social life flowed relatively uneventfully; he was not particularly attracted by the feats of decadent youth, which his schoolmates (students in Primorje developed all of a sudden, early) called fun. The idea of a beautiful book and music (he was already an accomplished pianist at the age of sixteen) tied him to the house. Still, Đuro's inner life was rich and diverse; although he had not experienced significant events, his youthful years were marked by profound crises that marked his later view of the world.

*

Two things tormented Đuro throughout his youth. At the age of twelve, when a conversation with older friends explained for the first time, quite clearly, what actually happens between husband and wife, the news shook his whole being. His mother, who cultivated him as a solitary plant, keeping the boy off the street, also instilled in him strong religious sentiments, which flourished even more under the increasingly accepted rites and perceived religious consolations. And the knowledge of this terrible secret, which—or so the boy thought—all people hide because it is a vile and dirty issue, this realization came just after his first Holy Communion, after the very day when Đuro believed he dwelt in the presence of angels. On the day of St. Aloysius, he walked in ecstasy with his companions through the portals of the ancient church, feeling the bliss of being in the presence of God.

Could this great, all-powerful, good God possibly tolerate such a horror? The act of procreation seemed to the young man to be the profanation of the soul, a stigma on humanity. A terrible fracture developed within him; for a moment, he—still a child—doubted the truth of a deity that had humiliated people with the original sin. "No, no—that can't be possible," he told himself, struggling to find corroboration from anyone that would show such a thing was indeed not possible. To ask one of his loved ones, he did not dare; it seemed to him that he would have to loathe his mother or move away if he were to learn that he actually had this act to thank for his existence. This was not because of the development of the first boyish signs of masculinity but rather because of a furious desire to prove both to his comrades and to his own ambivalence: "No, it is not so." He looked for books that had something to tell him about this.

He refused to believe statements that confirmed his doubts for a long time. For almost two years, there was a struggle in his soul between his thoughts of a heavenly, untainted life accomplished by people with a pure and good heart and the growing conviction that such a life was unattainable because our organism, divinely embodied, is subject to the laws of nature. And when he finally learned the truth from his sinful dreams and books, which he could not say were lying, all his religiosity turned into a youthful, truly devastating fantasy. He greedily read Büchner and similar books because it seemed to him that the two—God and our terrible nature—could not exist side by side. He began seeing his mother, relatives, and everyone with entirely different eyes. The words uttered by the priest about the majesty of the Savior's teaching, which once had had such a powerful hold over him, he now heard while aware of the ever-mocking refrain in his mind: "if it weren't for 'that thing'...."

And 'that thing' began calling him more powerfully. Meanwhile, he befriended a schoolmate, whom he considered an accomplished writer because some of his love songs had been published on the back pages of a local rag. He nearly fell in love with him and was influenced by his every word, following him like a faithful satellite. He then stumbled upon a book on sexual development, which stated that the first impulses usually occurred after this type of friendship; Đuro felt awful and began to withdraw from the world. He turned melancholic; having learned of the ordinary sin of youth, he began to doubt the value of life. He translated immature universal pain, so often borne of unspent youthful vigor, into misanthropy that somehow led him back to his lost

God. Religion, with its lofty thoughts of renunciation and purity, with a suffering Christ and an unblemished Virgin, compelled him again. When he first fell in love ('she' didn't even notice his love), he combined this love in his imagination with the thought of a pure, outward sentiment that had nothing to do with 'ordinary' human love.

For the first time, he accepted life and the idea of a god; the rules of this world no longer seemed terrible because—he thought—one could erase 'that thing' and, with angelic feelings, reach a loftier, more authentic meaning of life. The ideal of love did not suffer because his feelings remained unsettled and unreciprocated; the young man turned his troubles into verses and contented himself—when 'she' married in Trieste—with past memories of sweet moments spent with her.

At this time, he began to thirst for fame. His first literary achievements gave him a new direction. The thought of working for his homeland and family, which had previously agreed nicely with the outlook of a clean life spent for others, primarily for his neighbors, took a very specific form: to work in the literary field, to use the ubiquity and recognition of his work. With this new ideal, his old doubts completely disappeared; and so Đuro Andrijašević welcomed his eighteenth birthday with questions in his mind but also with much hope and faith in the value of his future works.

*

After graduating with top honors, he spent the holidays in Kraljevica at Uncle Toma's house. Like most folks in

Kraljevica, Toma rented rooms to beachgoers during the summer. That year, Miss Zora Marakova and her brother Marko, slightly younger than Andrijašević, lived in Toma's 'villa' (so-called because of a terrace at the main entrance and its location on a secluded hill). The two young men became fast friends and partook in outings and parties worth the time not spent on the beach. Miss Zora joined these excursions (fishing was of particular interest to her, as were other sports). After a few encounters, Ðuro started to feel that the girl's proximity had an unusual effect on him.

His impressions of women oscillated. On the one hand, was the beautiful, kind girl, worthy of pure love and devotion. He believed this to be true of almost every girl he had met. On the other hand, was the woman, the mother, generous and caring, and he, for the sake of her goodness of heart, should forget the uncomfortable 'thing' that made her a woman. Andrijašević read all he could learn about women of all kinds. He became aware of naturalist tendencies and became familiar with the concept of *'feminine'* in French comedy. But all this seemed more or less abstract; in his mind, he found—at least, so it appeared to him—only confirmations for his opinion. He was unhappy for a few days when he learned that his favorite author, Turgenev—creator of Liza, Jelena, and Gemma—had felt his best story to be *First Love*, in which Ðuro could make no sense of the character of Zinaida.

Zora Marakova was the daughter of a Czech immigrant, a factory manager in D. She was a handsome and angular girl with a sunburnt face and a sweet laugh. You could not call her beautiful, but—for her nineteen years—she was apt at joining parties and seeking company. Thanks to her transparent demeanor, she enchanted all those around her. She dressed elegantly and was always excited when something new, challenging and unusual occurred.

In the beginning, Đuro felt some antipathy towards her; in particular, he did not like her being so 'masculine' and independent when talking or acting. Instinctively, he felt this woman belonged to none of the categories he had in mind, so he didn't trust her.

Zora's sincerity quickly broke his distrust and timidity; Đuro agreed to take her fishing with her brother. At sea, at dawn, and while manning the oars, she was bright and cheerful as a bird; no misfortune could put off her good spirits (once after a storm, they were drenched; she liked the fact that they had to spend a few hours in a small fishing village and, to dry, changed into sailor suits—she chose huge nankeen pantaloons for herself). The Kajkavian dialect was a perfect match for her light-hearted banter. After several days, Đuro became accustomed to her calling him and Mark 'my boys' and did not get offended by the fact that when talking to him, she spoke as to a younger and inexperienced relation while his own mother and fellow professors treated him more formally. After all, they always talked about minutiae, fun, and play, so this familiar tone sounded to him perfectly natural.

On a late summer evening, all that changed. On the small terrace, they drank a home-brewed drink to celebrate Zora's birthday (Uncle Toma excused himself and went to the pub for a card game of *tresette*). A moon like that night, pouring its full light across Kvarner Bay, can be seen only from our southern shores. It was as if everyone felt that on such a lovely evening, soft and wide like quiet longing, the conversation should not be superficial; the partying mood was waning. Suddenly they all fell silent, and Zora, experiencing *deja vu*, said, "How wonderful it would be if we had someone who could read us a poem." After a few moments, she and her brother sat motionless, staring at the moonlight's reflection on the water, while listening to Đuro reading Heine's *Nordsee* in Croatian. The text was in Đuro's handwriting, and he admitted that this was his translation. The conversation shifted to literature; Zora knew surprisingly well the field Andrijašević loved. They sat on the terrace deep into the night, discussing new things they had never touched upon; the girl amazed Đuro with her deep insight and knowledge. For the first time, they didn't speak in dialect—and on the second day, the 'my boys' coming from Zora's mouth sounded strained. These were days when he and Zora completely forgot about Mark—days of shared reading and conversing, which ended, of course, with love.

This love was like a dream. The north wind *bura* whistled through the red caves by the sea, and Đuro followed Zora (he liked her tight-fitting suit of Styrian cloth with a man's cap so much!) along the steep pathways of a secluded, bare promontory by the sea. And then - the nights, the waning lascivious nights of summer on the coast, when the sea is sparkling and the air is shivering with lust! Marko had become ill with fever (in novices, a common illness from excessive bathing) so that the two of them could enjoy, virtually uninterrupted, the charm of unexpected love. September, a month of bloody and purple colors, when the evening sea is really—as Homer sings—like a glass of hot wine, bringing them the fear of their first parting...

Andrijašević did not dare leave his room the morning of his last day. He stayed up all night by candlelight, feeling devastated by the perversions of the previous evening. Disgusting, disgusting! he whispered to himself, struggling to find a stronger word. He, and only he, killed the great love so wonderfully surrounded by stunning natural beauty! And how could she lose her senses in the obscurity of the garden and forget the sanctity of their emotions? At that terrible hour, when they woke up no more as two ideal partners (as Đuro had always considered his love) but as humiliated humanity, an 'ordinary' husband and an 'ordinary' wife! He was close to running away, never to see her again—and when he finally came out and looked her in the eyes, he was appalled to see that she had no other sentiment for him but more of the same love. Thank God—she and her brother left on the third day; Đuro felt that if he had had to remain near her, he'd have to kill her and himself. For those two days, he felt awful. While preparing for his departure (he despised himself and hated her), Đuro became grief-stricken after finding that Uncle Toma had been severely ill all the time before Đuro's leaving for Vienna. Toma was suffering alone, having not seen even his mother, who arrived later from Rijeka, fearing for his life.

He got out of bed debilitated and wanted only to depart; he anxiously waited for the day he had to leave for Vienna to register at the university. Each, sometimes intimate, living memory of his past love, every pebble, fragrant plant on the hill recently plucked for her as an ornament, the stone table on the terrace—witness of the timid first longings, all this vexed him to tears.

And he, all by himself, had to destroy all of it! He knew he wasn't consciously guilty of anything, but this realization worsened the pain. And hating the world, her, everything he had believed in earlier, so engrossed him that when her first letter arrived, he sat at the table and feverishly wrote her a few pages, practically cursing while at the same time grieving with self-pity. And after receiving no answer to that letter, he almost sighed in relief as if he had escaped a terrible nightmare.

At first, he felt too weak to think about how to deal with her, but when he tried to pour out all his sadness in a poem in which he wanted to tell everyone how low and weak they were, he felt for the first time that he had no faith in the written word. He wrote several pages, crossed them out ten times over, and stopped; "it's all just a declaration and a statement that can't erase what really happened," he said to himself, ripping up the scribbled sheets. For the first time, he suspected that literature added little value to life—and that doubt never really left him.

*

His self-control, the confidence of relentless young enthusiasm, was forever gone. In the metropolis, Andrijašević morphed into an entirely different man. Behind the first onslaught of pain for the pathetic end of this second love came repentance. He waited for days and days for a reply from Zora. Their passion could not end like this. He felt attached to the girl who might have become his wife, yet he did not know how to fix the mistakes he had written in the dizziness of the first disappointment. Zora did not reply. He felt that her love had turned into contempt, that she thought of him as a coward, a weakling, who had withdrawn when the moment for serious obligations arose. He was looking for a way to write at least to her brother Mark—but couldn't make up his mind. There came months of despair in which he joined the worst student groups and started to become an utterly dissolute man. His life began to move within the narrow, boring boundaries of endless sleepless nights and lazily mediocre days. Abusing his nerves, he lost interest in science and began to look for ways to demean himself further, deceiving himself that he was not worthy of being alive. A year passed in a mental fog, lifting for a moment when the thought "Zora will write to me anyway" would dawn. He did not give himself an account of what would happen if she did and how their relationship would develop, but he felt he could not live with that burden on his soul. But—Zora did not write.

He couldn't even learn her whereabouts. He tried this: he beautifully described his suffering. The literary success was great—but it did not ease his misery. Zora did not reply to that painful call either. He did not rush home for the holidays, fearing that his mother and Uncle Toma had heard about his present life. At the end of the third semester, he found himself in the company of old buildings, feeling old, failed, incapable of any decision, and wounded in body and soul.

Those days were ugly. There were also material worries, unpaid bills, his hiding in remote Viennese areas, and his shame with his mates. "To end it, to end it all" —he uttered this thought almost daily, to switch into a complete apathy, not even answering his mother's letters. He avoided his fellow students and started searching for company in peripheral establishments, meeting places for low-income folks. He felt comfortable being treated as a "doctor" (in Vienna, every student is a doctor for the landlady and the waiter; when he earned his doctorate, he was promoted to 'professor'), appreciated, and listened attentively. In the summer of his second year, he did not enroll in the university, convincing himself that "it's all the same anyway." He got used to long nights in muddy locales amongst drunkards, and, at least to some extent, alcohol soothed him. The role of a desperado became second nature to him—and with almost declamatory gestures, he began to get drunk night after night, worrying only about how he would spend the next day without getting bored. He'd get up after midday, dine, and lay down again until evening, finding the time to read whatever would come to him. A few times, he tried to write, to create. The conviction of the futility of it so preoccupied him that he soon chucked his pen and, in an even more miserable mood, went to the inn to drown his anguish in liquor.

He was afraid of only one thing: his mechanical life would have to change by going back home or seeing one of his friends. He learned to avoid meeting those who had known him before, making it clear how deeply and permanently he had gone downhill. "Wait till the end," he buried all his former intentions with that thought.

Before the holidays, he received a letter from his mother that Uncle Toma was demanding to see him. He would, under no circumstances, send him money to stay in Vienna for the summer.

After delaying for as long as he could, he left for home at the end of July. Mrs. Andrijašević greeted her son with joy and without asking unpleasant questions. Still, Đuro suddenly realized that she had aged dramatically, probably because of her presentiments about his student life. She had become more religious; she and Uncle Toma seemed to be waiting for him to say something, to explain what he had been doing for two years. On the third evening, when he and his uncle had long conversations that had not yet touched on his lifestyle in Vienna, he noticed that his mother quietly carried a third bottle of wine to the table. The same night, he left home, wrote a letter to Toša, a friend from elementary school with whom he had corresponded, and asked to be invited under any pretext; in eight days, Đuro traveled to the village in Podravina where Toša's parents had their estate.

*

In the countryside, surrounded by people who knew from Toša's accounts only the best about him, Andrijašević felt that his will to live was returning after a long time. Respect for the hosts (Toša had a widowed father and an aunt who ran the household) made him shed his sedentary habits. He got up early and demonstrated interest in Toša's father's farm, the evening routine of enjoying drink too much spontaneously waned. Toša immediately noticed Đuro's significant change over the last two years, so—first jokingly and then seriously—he began poking him about his having abandoned literary work altogether. One night, Andrijašević revealed everything to his friend, who had charmed him from the very time they'd shared a school bench with his cheerful and sunny temperament; Đuro confessed the nature of his misery.

"You, the gray hawk, experienced a tiny setback in love and immediately cried like a baby. Eh, poet, look at yourself! If only you wanted to listen to me, I would prescribe you a cure right away: start working for me or my father (Toša graduated, attended a course in economics for a year, and returned home to help his father), and you will see the melancholy disappear.

"You're talking like a farmer. Do you think this romantic disappointment (Đuro had given him just a quick overview of the affair with Zora) is the cause of all this misery? It is not, my dear; it has a deeper root: why do anything and strain yourself when you cannot face even the simplest of life's problems! I played chess for days and days in Vienna—in truth, it made the time pass by, and it took away the time to think about my anguish; but knowing that, you're not going to claim that playing chess has solved the question of the reason for my existence. And your work and my chess are of equal value if you look carefully."

"You forget that life is not easy. Okay: something unpleasant happened to you. So you lost energy, lost two years, started to drink. Let it be. But do you think unhappiness is the only thing that will happen in your life? Look: in the last two years, your novel was published (even peasants, as you may see, have interests), giving you name recognition. You have a mother and an uncle who are waiting for you; also—do you think it is a minor sin that you'd be deceiving all of us who expected something great from you? Just remember how we, as students, accepted every newly published work and tracked every progress of our writers. Think: How many young hearts are waiting for you to continue—and how many look at you as our future novelist? You're too self-centered, that's all."

"No, no—I just can't. My determination and enthusiasm cannot settle down here."

"You're cheating yourself. You say you spent all your days in Vienna sleeping, and behold, here you already starting to make sense of my father's business."

The consequence of all these conversations was that Đuro followed Toša's advice and enrolled in the third year at the University of Zagreb.

*

After a few months, the daily Zagreb newspaper published reviews and criticisms signed by "Đ.A." This rapidly led to the recognition of their merit; the leading literary newspaper began publishing "a novel by Đ. Andrijašević."

But the turning point was not only Toša's work; Đuro was inspired by something completely different.

Fugue

The widow of Major R., who rented him a room in Zagreb, found room in his apartment for a piano, even though the place was already too crowded (after retiring, she could not afford a large flat but did not want to give away her things for free); the piano, on which her daughters had practiced until leaving for a convent school in Carniola. At first, Ðuro would only occasionally open the old instrument, whose keys had already been softened. Before long, he regretted what he had forgotten after not practicing for two years and started playing regularly, until finally enrolling in the class of a well-known music teacher in Zagreb. The teacher, living only for music, gladly welcomed this man who, despite being somewhat older, was still willing to wrestle with the torments of practicing; he loved Andrijašević very much. He introduced him to his more advanced students in three months and into a group whose most important concern was arranging musical 'five o'clocks.' Thus, Ðuro Andrijašević was introduced to the home of Hrabar, a senior government official. Or should we say to his wife's home, since Hrabar spent all his time in a tavern playing tarok, leaving his daughter Vera entirely in Mrs. Nina's care?

It took Andrijašević some time to feel comfortable around them. During his two Viennese years—he had let himself go and tended to become shy when dealing with people of higher social standing. And the Hrabar family—that is, the mother and daughter—were in the top thousand of the capital.

In the last years of the past century, Zagreb developed an unusual social structure. It was a city of academic excellence, important offices, all kinds of schools, the center of all cultural life, and a town with the cream of the crop in brainpower. These gave the outward veneer of a metropolis, which makes itself felt when one visits an inn, a café, the ice rink, and the fashionable seasonal dances. In reality, the centralization of these intellectuals was more the result of rail transport than spontaneous development. There was a growing mismatch between the vital needs of this *intelligentsia* and its economic power. The burghers, who alone could have constituted a solid base for this rapid progress, remained *purgars* confined to Vlaška and lower Ilica, still seeking and finding entertainment and company in time-honored pubs. But the son of this burgher often turned into someone with a very Western European need for sophisticated culture, and his daughter even more so. This is how a peculiar female type developed: a girl who learned nothing about the demands of higher society at a young age; her schooling, language skills, and natural gifts made it easier for her to follow an ideal, keeping her apart from her dear and kind mother who nevertheless remained the pillar of the family and an eternal guardian angel—but could not write in skinny and spiky letters according to English fashion, and often understood almost nothing of the topics of conversation occurring in a theater foyer or at a house party.

This was, essentially, her *mamica*, Mrs. Nina Hrabar. She had married her husband thirty years before, consenting to live in his native town where they were transferred; she never embraced Zagreb's spirit. Vera was already a product of that spirit; a talented girl, she graduated from gymnasium, learned to speak three foreign languages fluently, played the piano very well for an amateur, and knew how to conduct a conversation in society flawlessly. Recently, two or three schoolmistresses from England arrived in Zagreb, and these became a model of *comme il faut* for Vera and her girlfriends. Life's top priorities were education and refined manners in the young women's world. Occasionally, one could hear reflections of northern European demands for women's independence, but the average aspirations for the female generation were more modest and indecisive, especially in the essentials, in the relationship between husband and wife; when faced with questions of marriage, all these otherwise worldly and seemingly self-confident ladies acted like children, confusing betrothal, matrimony, and marriage, treating all of these as exercises in etiquette, most of all as something that comes with age, like the first dance.

After the early encounters, Andrijašević could still not understand Vera. More by instinct, he felt that this 'virgin' (in his mind, he always assumed her to be one) was far from the abyss he had thrust himself into after breaking up with Zora. Their breakup was now only a distant memory. Still, the belief that life in its entirety is sordid and ugly, reinforced by the reading of natural science books that exposed the truth about man-animal without an ascertainable question—this belief so pervaded him, that Vera was an almost incomprehensible being. And her looks—a tall, skinny girl with golden hair and calm green eyes—were quite in tune with his impression of a virginal and unblemished woman.

"And to think that for two years in Vienna I have not spoken to a woman, except to waitresses or streetwalkers!" he would think with bitterness as he was always afraid of hurting Vera's 'holy' being by the utterance of an offensive word or otherwise by his social clumsiness. At a musical soiree, she was asked what she thought of Anna Karenina; he was almost embarrassed that Vera wanted to read that book and told her the book might hurt her soul.

"I'm no longer the little girl you think I am!"

"Every great book depicts life; if one can't stand the writer's emotions, one should not read books."

"In other words: serious literature is only for such serious and gloomy men as yourself, and we—immature girls—should always stick with Andersen. How old do I need to be?—I'm quite old already."

"Age is not measured by years but by the winters of life." (Đuro understood that he was using a stereotype and blushed). "We'd better not talk about this, Miss; I don't want to be the first to provoke your interest in venturing out into such a winter. (The flush on his face, he felt, was growing stronger). I express myself awkwardly, but our carefree afternoon with a piano is more valuable than reading any serious books."

*

After this conversation, Vera became interested in this young gentleman who, in her opinion, had until then made the unforgivable mistake of not wanting to dance; he also always spoke casually. It annoyed her to be considered 'stupid.' So, to pay him back, she would viciously mention all his mistakes, his laziness, or even the slightest social *faux pas* like the somewhat comical severity in criticizing one of Vera's friends who interpreted a mazurka by Chopin as a dance, even though it was written just before Chopin died. She decided to read Tolstoy's novel 'right now,' and at the first opportunity, asked her teacher (with whom—from childhood, as his best student—she was used to talking openly): "what kind of man is this Andrijašević?" The teacher praised Đuro's intelligence and said, "It just seems that he is too old for his age." That aroused Vera's interest even more, and at the first opportunity, she told Đuro her impressions of the book. For fear that it would not be acceptable to engage with a man in a conversation dealing with the underpinnings of ordinary social relations and also her desire to see how Andrijašević would speak about the same subject in front of a crowd, Vera ventured to talk about Tolstoy in front of everyone. In this group, there were many music enthusiasts, including Professor M., who constantly harassed Mrs. Nina for not forcing her daughter into a full-fledged piano career; G., a young lawyer and distant relative of the Hrabars, in love with Miss Milka (the one who did not understand Chopin); Miss Milka and two of Vera's classmates, one of them a very emancipated woman, a college graduate, a school teacher, always ready to cross spears in favor of Ellen Key's ideas; finally two older ladies who were discussing with the hostess what dances to attend while allowing the youngsters to have fun at will.

Mr. M. could not even hear Tolstoy's name without going up in flames; he could never forgive the Russian apostle for the denunciations of Beethoven and for writing *Kreutzer's Sonata*. So he immediately jumped on Tolstoy, attesting that there was nothing artistic about the book *Anna Karenina*. Vera half-heartedly defended Tolstoy (the novel greatly impressed her, but she could hardly tell why). When she began to exalt the figure of Kitty Shtcherbatsky, she turned to Đuro, who was following the conversation in silence, for support and help.

"With regard to the figure of Katerina and Levin, I would almost agree with the professor. Tolstoy was affected by his bias and perhaps by memories from his past."

"Are the figures of Katarina and Levin from real life?" asked the emancipated lady importantly.

"Artists never copy reality. Not even when this is their artistic gospel; but Tolstoy says somewhere that the scene where Levin and Kitty come to an understanding in the garden was inspired by real-life experience: this was truly how Tolstoy revealed his love to his wife. And besides, these are side issues; the prophet Tolstoy— when describing Levin and his wife, the primary artistic purpose for Tolstoy was to describe Anna and her love. And in those descriptions there is poetry, even music, although this angers the Professor." Đuro smiled. She and Karenin are alive just then.

"And Vronsky?" (Vera disliked Vronsky and felt a strong antipathy).

"I don't understand Vronsky. I appreciate his later actions and the development of his love for Anna; these are clear to me, but I do not understand the beginning of that love. Vronsky's soul is foreign and impenetrable to me."

The conversation drifted spontaneously to men's ideals, to love, women. After a long time, Andrijašević felt comfortable listening to his own words, almost forgot his timidity, and began to describe, in broad strokes, with strong words, the ideal woman in this Russian work, which was his favorite. The conversation ended in dissonance, as everyone felt that Andrijašević was better at expressing his views, that they could not match his skill. The women felt the discourse too serious, while both men, the professor and the lawyer, felt malice and anger.

That night Vera couldn't sleep. She was surprised that this evening she had noticed how beautiful was Andrijašević's facial expression. How bright were his eyes! How clearly he could present his thoughts! Really—not an ordinary fellow. And oddly enough, he does not like that unfriendly Vronsky either!

"Vera, you can't sleep, eh?"

"No, Mother."

"It's all of those intellectual diatribes. Andrijašević spoiled the whole party today. I saw the professor get angry."

"It is not Andrijašević's fault that the other two did not have what it takes or did not know how to defend their thoughts."

Mrs. Hrabar was astonished at her daughter's resolute voice, but her drowsiness kept her from dwelling on this any further.

*

Đuro spent the following three weeks in great internal turmoil. He became more and more apt at denying his closeness to Vera; by the very talk of Tolstoy, he understood that only in him was she seeking support, that she was drinking in his words. In the days that followed, the invisible bond between the two grew, and Đuro's dead, dormant heart started waking, beating stronger, and rushing towards meeting 'her.'

"I love her, I love her!" he shouted to himself, and he didn't let a sunny day go by without going out to see nature (the same fellow who had literally drowned in café life); he felt as if he were a part of the dewy grass, the broad shadows, and the chirping flocks.

But after sunny days came the fog (the spring was slow that year), and there were muddy, chilly mornings with snow drifting along the sidewalks and vapors rising from dark green pools of water.

Andrijašević's boldness and enthusiasm were suddenly lost; he would convince himself that he was too old and sinful for this new, great love; he was incapable of erasing the past that made him unworthy of Vera's love. Twice, he did not show up at a party; afterward, he noticed a reproachful look in Vera's eyes. He felt like a scarecrow surrounded by his memories. When he noticed a change in Mrs. Nina's behavior (the caring mother had quickly guessed that her daughter's calm heart was troubled) and felt her unfriendly greeting like a blow, he retired to his room. He took to his bed for three days, constantly repeating the same phrase, "How dare you, a corrupt, vicious man, encroach like a criminal on her inaccessible world! Who gives you the right to disturb the tranquility of the soul of this virginal girl?"

Those doubts turned into a poem, the most recent that Đuro sent to print. It portrays Vera as a royal dignitary, dormant for a hundred years in a magic garden. He, a knight, comes from an unknown world of violence, blood, abduction and sin and stands behind the hedge surrounding her garden, breaking his bloody sword, not daring to rush to her...

When the poem was published (he knew Vera would read it immediately), he was almost afraid to see her. Although he had spelled out his confession in the lyrics, he feared that Vera would actually understand its meaning. He wished to go home, leave Zagreb, stay away from her, smother his love in the bud—and there he was surprised by a letter from the music teacher, a summon to come to visit.

The teacher handed him a note, as if by accident, with this text:

"I know You may find it strange, perhaps too bold, to write to You. I must speak to You, but I found no better way than this to ask You to visit on Thursday. V."

The letter "V"—the beginning of the name—explained everything to Đuro. How many times did he kiss the expensive paper with its undefined smell! "Beloved holy virgin!" he kept repeating in a light fog of happiness, not thinking about what was to come.

On Thursday, a sizable crowd welcomed Andrijašević at the Hrabars, but Vera was absent. She used some urgent purchases as an excuse (Đuro immediately realized the reason for her act: she was ashamed and afraid of the present day, dear girl!) and came only later, flushed as if she had been walking from afar. Đuro immediately noticed the deep rings beneath her eyes and was over-whelmed by compassion; he felt tears streaming from his eyes. But Vera's general behavior was, that very day, unfriendly and almost cold; she did not seem to notice him and tortured him with her excessive attentiveness to the other guests.

Professor M. sat down at the piano, signaling that the general conversation should stop. The evening's shad-ows descended, but no one asked to turn on the lights, focusing on the performance. Dvorak's *Legends* was the ideal night music.

After the last chords, the company gathered around the player and asked him loudly for an encore. Vera took that opportunity to come very close to Andrijašević.

"I was wrong to write to You. If You want to fix our situation, I ask that You forget my message."

Andrijašević looked straight at her. Her features were not recognizable in the twilight; but he saw well that she had no strength to withstand his gaze. At once, as if some magic wand had suddenly changed him, he was overcome by anger, pride, and bile. He thought he could, without a problem, take her hands, squeeze her wrists, and enjoy her pain. A strange voice, never heard before, came from his throat; as if he were not the speaker but a Mephistopheles, cold, measured, with a hint of amusement:

"You can count on my discretion. We probably won't see each other again; I am leaving Zagreb."

Her eyes look at him, blinking, brimming with tears.

"Why did you write that!"

All her shame, love, and fear for what she discovered reduced to the simple problem of a knight afraid to awaken a queen.

There was no time for an answer; the others brought candles, and the two were reabsorbed in the group. Andrijašević was barely aware of what was going on that evening. He remembered leaving, escaping from the acquaintances and drifting to a long street ending in an open field. He recalled later that somewhere near the Sava River, he was sitting in a small, empty tavern; he then returned to his apartment in darkness (he knew there was still a play ongoing at the theater), lay down on the sofa, and cried, as children cry, choking with tears that could not be rationalized.

When he calmed down, he lit the lamp, and with tremendous effort (blood pounded in his temples because of nerves and the wine, so he kept pressing his forehead with his hands), he began writing her a letter on the first piece of paper that came to his hands. "Vera! I am mad and committing a crime, but it cannot remain like this between us....."

He kept writing to her about everything; his life, lethargic and dead, was built on a colossal disappointment, his love for her, and his fear of that love.

When he had finished, he sealed the letter and, not thinking whether he should do so, went to the café, bought a stamp, and threw the letter into the mailbox.

Addressed straight to Vera.

He wandered from one café to another all night, went to the station early in the morning, and took the first train to a village near Zagreb. Returning home that night, he was shattered and cold-hearted and learned from the landlady that a clerk had left a letter for him. He found, in an envelope with the teacher's monogram scribbled by her—apparently very quickly—the words:

"If You believe I can be a comfort for Your pain, I am ready."

This transformed Andrijašević into another man—

***

Đuro remembers all this while gazing at his surroundings, morphed by the trains' speed into a monotonous mass of branches and walls. Remembering his first acquaintance with Vera, he is happy and pleased to think, "After all, she is my girl!"—words that always come to his mind when he hears something nice about her.

People gathered their baskets and suitcases; the train soon stopped.

Toša welcomed his friend.

"Great idea! And you will be happy with us; my wife could not come to welcome you; we have a two-year-old daughter whom we cannot leave alone."

"And your old man?"

"Still the same. He won't forgive me. It was not easy to argue with him, and it was nicer at home than here in Zdenci; but what am I to do, the old man was fixated that I should marry Dikić's daughter; he was obsessed by the idea of merging two neighboring properties. I could not abandon my Anka so I became a teacher. It would be difficult without my mother's help, but the way it is now - there is enough of everything in the house, Anka and I are both happy with each other and happy with our little Micika, so what more do you want!"

At the inn of the train station, Andrijašević quickly ate something and sent Vera a short note, that he would "write more soon." After a brief interval (Toša obviously had a hard time staying away from home, so he didn't even want to cross the bridge to have a look at the Bosnian side), the car started.

Chapter II

In Zdenci, on the 5th of November

And so, now I'm keeping a diary. I could never understand the point of writing one's own thoughts and feelings in a book not intended for anyone to read. If you know that someone will be able to peek into your soul and put it on paper, I think it will be impossible for you to write a journal without inhibitions. Should you talk to yourself—thoughts convey more meaning and fly faster than a pen will ever be able to do.

When a girl writes a diary about her first love, it is because of the understandable need to communicate happiness or sadness when they are too big. But why should I speak to myself in a way that can never be as honest and sincere as pure introspection?

I don't know where to start—I just want to kill time. Toša's family goes to bed with the chickens; after being here for eight days, I still can't get used to that. I try to shorten the long evenings by reading (in the countryside, winter must be categorically terrible; winter is more fitting as a depiction of death than sleep—ha, a catchphrase!); country winters hurt my eyes. I can't write or start any literary work; it's a no-go. November is not my month—and besides, nothing in this village's life would interest me to the point of being willing to recreate it.

After all, it's a bad sign that I started writing these letters to myself. Three months ago, I would often sit down at my desk and write to Vera: not a letter, but an endless dream, a tumultuous fantasy on paper. Why have I forgotten that today and am no longer speaking—to her?

I feel a little angry: it has already been five days since I heard from her. Nothing. Is she offended? I do not believe so; I explained the whole thing to her in a letter: that when passing through Zagreb, I would be visiting them anyway. It will be soon, and I will immediately reserve a seat.

Only—is the reason for her silence that I must find a job? I don't want to think about that. Today, I'm not in the best mood. And when a good disposition is missing, the philosopher is ready to turn around his optimistic method.

The village is still—I have never heard such profound silence. Alas!—I cannot write. It always comes to mind that this is a failed academic exercise. If only I could have something lighter to read; I never thought that newspapers would be necessary. And now that I have begun to take an interest in our politics, there is none of that here!

*

November the 7th

When I went to sleep last night, I remembered a strange fellow in Bourget's *Cosmopolis*. My colleague, writer Julien Dorsenne. He goes around the world, notebook in hand, and captures impressions and memories—and then later throws them into his novels. That ought to be the way to justify my scribblings.

But this Dorsenne is a little comical. Anyway, today's conversation with Toša is worth writing about.

We were talking about the village. I have never seen an authentic village or a real peasant who knows only his land. The people of Primorje, even when they are tending a vineyard, are not peasants (and probably never were); their occupation changes as needed: at a young age, they might be a sailor, later they make their living on board their boat or by working around the vineyards. They are always ready to come up with something better.

Here, I was making the acquaintance of the true peasant. All that matters to him is dictated by mother earth, our provider. No wonder this man cannot stand schools; he sees no connection between the written word and works in the fields. And that, being distrustful of folks from the city, it seems to me, is not only due to the alleged negligence by urban dwellers or the dominance of urban notaries. My Pajo or Nicholas does not understand why the "townie" even exists; since it is not evident to him that life can even exist without soil, he holds true to a societal organization provided by an unjust fate that is not attractive to him.

Toša turned the conversation to literature and we immediately started to argue.

"You all complain that our books don't sell well, that writers are suffering. I buy almost every Croatian book; so do you know what is wrong with everything here? You fellows are awfully weak; you don't believe in yourselves or anyone else; you always describe anxious and tormented individuals. And look at the two of us here; what are we doing? I can't figure out your artistic strategy; how will you attract the masses?" (Toša is all fierce in the debate, which fits him perfectly; his Anka idolizes him).

"You, Toša, have failed to see that most people do not understand us because they do not read us or cannot read. And if there were fewer analphabets, even your farmer from Zdenci would have some interest in a beautiful book."

"Our people are backward, true, but why is it that a Czech who settled here reads and even buys books?"

"He has greater spiritual needs; when he understands us, our man will cease to be the peasant he is today."

"And now all your work is pointless?"

"It is not. We are a small nation, and this is why the writer cannot find many people to dialog with. Besides, we are a people made for farming, and it is difficult for us to be culturally enlightened. In my opinion, a growing number of booksellers and all other outward signs of an expanding cultural life are possible only in a nation that has already completed that first stage and has embarked on industrialization. You know what? There are more books and newspapers in Czechia today than in Italy, although the cultural difference is enormous. This is all because Italy lags behind the Czech lands in terms of industrial growth."

"But that's no way to fix a thing! You will continue describing your depressing characters, and we will feel optimistic and not understand you; you will be starving, and we will have nothing to read!"

"We write how we feel. If I were to, for example, describe such an ideal cheerful male as you, I would struggle: the portrait would come out badly, so it would not interest anyone."

"But think—people want to believe, and they are waiting for your uplifting and courageous work."

"Toša, you are using a big word: *People*! Here are your people for you. I am no different; I love their *kolo* dance (although they often sing terribly indecent lyrics); I enjoy hearing these songs. I know that nowhere could I feel as happy as when I am among our people; I have a lot of old-fashioned love for our country, our native land, but, brother, you will also admit that we are, compared to them, only poets and romantics. What do these 'people' you live with daily know about Croatia? Their world ends with the boundaries of the village—at most, they go to Slavonski Brod. And Zagreb—our other brothers, those at the other end—what do they know about it all?"

"Teach them, so they learn." (Toša forgot that he had told me the day before that it was nearly impossible for rural children to think in geographical terms.)

"You said it was hard to teach at school; and what will be later taught by our politicians—stay away from that, brother!"

That is how we came to politics, and Toša almost cursed me because I am altogether uninterested in it. I told him he didn't have a single newspaper at home; and, you bet, today I see that he has borrowed a whole bundle of old newspapers from the vicar in another village.

What a great fellow! A man so full of joy and courage that it is a delight to behold. His Anka seems made just for him. She is fresh, beautiful, and not as dowdy as many of our women. There is only one thing on her mind: her husband and Micika and maybe a larger family, which is sure to come.

And she's modest, by God! For the life of me, I cannot imagine Vera living in this desolate village.

*

November the 8th

Everything is habit. Today it feels weird to go to bed without putting anything in writing in these notes.

Vera wrote to me. Oh, my wonderful girl! How simply yet powerfully does she express her thoughts. A few words—and they say so much, so much!

She writes: "I trust you completely, and what you have decided, I believe, is certainly the best for all."

Tonight I was looking at her photo. Has anything changed lately?

Wilde's Dorian Gray looks at his portrait and sees when the oil-painted canvas changes. The idea is perverse but beautiful. If there were no end, where Wilde kills his hero "through the canvas," I would argue that the fantastic Englishman wanted to say that we can find everything we want in a single picture.

The truth is: Vera's eyes today look at me from her photo with great confidence.

She *is* my girl, after all!

*

I don't feel like adding the date anymore because it seems that Toša and his sleepiness will impel me to write my impressions every day.

November, December, and January; I will definitely get a job in February. And the exam? I should take it as soon as possible.

It was stupid not to bring any books with me. It would be great to read here.

As far as my inertia goes, I am generally a lazy fellow—I liked to sit in the Arkadencafé in Vienna all day and stare at nothing, thinking about nothing. Vera was angry at me when I once said that the couch was one of the greatest inventions of modern times.

I have the whole day here to rest, yet this does not do the trick for me. It is as if laziness is only sweet if one really has something relevant to do.

You can see that Vera's letter made me happy. Today, I'd almost like to start a project, write stories, anything. Inspiration is an odd phenomenon. In Vienna, so many times during the first year, I took a pen in my hand, struggled, made a real effort—and never finished writing anything! Sometimes you just cannot command words—you can't find the phrases; the writing says something other than what you wanted it to say.

And in that beautiful spring when Vera and I met—how easy things were then! I was almost capable of capturing thoughts with my pen—everything seemed easy, and it was always so easy to find the right words; they came spontaneously.

Those were great times. There had never been so much desire in me for life. How beautifully all the pieces fell together one after another, success upon success. In summer, I was already part of the cream of the crop of our writers—and everything seemed so good, so perfectly in place!

Indeed, success is wonderful. I know that with the applause of the audience in the theater (when will I dare again to write a drama?), I forgot our creed that, first of all, we must understand "the tastes of our public."

Now I need something like that. I'm a little anxious about moving to a provincial town - and becoming a teacher.

Hmm—I've never really considered that. Oh well, I have all the time in the world for this!

Good night, Vera—all will be well!

November the 11th

I didn't think I would be so affected by this news. I open a stack of the newspapers that the pastor sends to Toša, and by strange coincidence, a name pops out.

I read: Appointments and reassignments. Zora Marak, a teacher in a gymnasium for girls—was reassigned to a yet higher-level school in V.

So—that's what happened with Zora! A teacher— educating children eventually will turn into an old maid in an empty home.

What has she been doing? How has she been living this past six years? Has she forgotten me completely— and has she made her peace?

I feel very, very guilty. If she kept alive the memory of our love—as it certainly appears because she has not married, she became a teacher—that must be torturing her. It's sad even to think about it.

And nothing anymore, nothing can be repaired. What would it mean if I wrote to her...

No, no, that thought is completely cruel. And I can't because of Vera. After all, maybe she is satisfied with her calling.

Why did I have to get to know her on my journey and then so stupidly split with her?

My life has so far depended on women. Is it because we romantics, we sensitive types, feel love so intensely?

And what about the big ideas? How little truth is there in what philosophers say! They speak of the state of the world, good and evil, and forces and imperatives—all of which are ultimately nothing but the consequence of the temperaments and impressions of us, the living.

I was desperate after the business with Zora. It made me understand Nietzsche's anarchist thought of suicide (the superhuman sacrifices himself, renouncing human- ity), while Schopenhauer annoyed me with his approach to art. Everything looked black—disheartening.

After meeting Vera, I quickly changed. Yes, the past remains within us somewhat. It binds us and captures us, but for the time being, I agree with the ancient Greeks who wanted to interpret everything in terms of black and white bile.

When our philosophy is genuinely stable, and we pursue a constant direction and view on life, youth and development cease. What takes over is indifference to life that can be defined by "absolutely true" ideas. Where did this come from?—from Zora!

November the 12th

Family life is a beautiful thing. In it, small, insignificant events that otherwise go unnoticed gain special significance. Toša and Anka merely live as two, but lunch, dinner, and a walk—all these mean far more to them than they do to a bachelor. In would never occur to me to sit at a table with such a ceremony, drink coffee and attend Sunday social calls!

They do this with a perpetually happy smile. This is how little it takes to find happiness! Toša is a teacher with a salary of thirty forints, from his family money maybe another sixty. Yet they live like nobility.

I never thought life in the country would be so inexpensive. Maybe because there is not much of an opportunity to spend anything. But we, in the city—now that's another story. Toša's wife would die of boredom if she weren't doing household chores, cooking and cleaning all day long, and doing them happily.

It occurred to me today that this could be Vera standing in the kitchen, yelling at Micika to stay away from the stove. I laughed; that's crazy, absurd, I cannot imagine it.

*

Today I don't even know the date. The Turks say days go by slowly and the years pass quickly. Anyway, I am here for the third week and have not yet begun to make a plan. I ought to write to Vera - and submit my petition, but nothing.

There is still time for the petition. If only I knew where they would send me.

*

November the 16th

A little avalanche is rolling down the hill. Well, I knew things couldn't stay quiet forever.

Today I got a letter from old Mrs. Hrabar. Indeed, this whole thing appears to be very important to her; as far as I know, it takes her a very long time before writing to anyone. Vera used to tell me that one must keep track of relatives instead of letting mother do it.

That's what she writes. She invites me to come to visit Zagreb as soon as possible because she has—she says—important matters to discuss.

Are these signs of a storm?

What may have happened?

Vera's letter was so full of confidence—without accusatory tones. And between the lines, the old lady blames me for not coming to visit them immediately.

To me, all the preparations that precede a marriage have forever seemed very dull. The formal proposal, engagement, wedding, and so forth

It will be worse for me; I also ought to attend church consultations. Well—we will.

Chapter III

———

"Ivan, there is something I wish to discuss."

Advisor Hrabar looks at his wife and is surprised. They get along well enough: he lives according to his habits; she takes care of Vera and the house. For years, communications with his wife has concerned well-defined and predictable things: the monthly contribution for the house (Hrabar needs relatively little for himself), the incidentals with the landlord, and the procurement of wine (Hrabar always sees to that). Not much needs to be said about these minutiae. When household expenses go up because of Vera, so does Hrabar's salary—so it will be difficult for Hrabar to conceive of an unexpected event, a greater need for money, or something that might force him to address his wife differently than usual.

Something had happened—no doubt. Hrabar was in a hurry to leave for the café, but still not wanting to admit it, replied with a shaky voice:

"Need we talk now?"

"The sooner, the better. That's why I sent Vera to the Golubićes."

"I'm ready, my dear."

Mrs. Nina went to the door quite theatrically and opened it as if she had caught someone eavesdropping. She did not usually put on airs, but now it seemed that doing this would somehow increase the significance of what she was about to say to her husband.

Mr. Hrabar rolled a cigarette and waited.

"The matter is very serious. We have not so far talked about it; I have not told you anything, although more than once I wished to. It concerns Vera's marriage."

"What, did Andrijašević…?"

Mrs. Hrabar abruptly interrupts her husband.

"What do you think—that he has abandoned her? How can you think such a thing? I would never let matters get that far. If this relationship needs dissolving, we will do it, not he, no, never!"

"So—you want it dissolved, do you?"

"Listen. Three weeks ago, Andrijašević wrote to Vera that he had taken the final oral exams but could not take the professor's exam because he had no money. Early on, he always spoke of a rich uncle" (he did only once, after she asked him, but now Mrs. Hrabar felt some joy in smearing Đuro's name), "and that was why I indulged her and agreed to this half-baked engagement; now he writes that this uncle died, leaving him nothing."

"Well, the young man will take the exam …"

"What are you thinking, please! 'Take the exam!'" she imitated her husband. "My dear, that exam takes a year, maybe even two. And Vera has now reached the age of twenty-five. Twenty-five plus two equal twenty-seven. Professor M. told me the situation is so bad that even

54

after the exam, he will still have to wait to receive a salary. That comes to twenty-eight."

"They have waited so long..."

"Yeah, but this is too long. And what would we do if he leaves her in the end? We are not rich, and Vera is a proud girl. An only child should not be left so lightly to her destiny. In short: I have thought a great deal about this, and in the end, I wrote to Andrijašević to come for a visit. So I wanted to warn you not to be too kind or friendly with him if you meet him before I do."

"And our little girl?" (Hrabar always called Vera a *little girl* even though she was already an adult).

"Leave that to me. I want the two of us to be clear about this."

"Very well, dear. Just don't upset your child without reason."

Mr. Hrabar stands up, kisses his wife, which he rarely does, and goes to his pub.

*

Mrs. Hrabar did not tell her husband the whole story: more importantly, she did not tell him that it was her firm intention to undo their engagement by whichever means necessary and as soon as possible. "This is not a proper engagement; everything happened out of order with this Andrijašević. It is as if we should be ashamed that Vera *is* engaged. He didn't even propose, she told me herself. It is best that we have kept everything secret and haven't printed announcements."

Đuro had never been Mrs. Hrabar's favorite. She understood that he was very well educated, she heard his praise sung, and she was at the theatre when Đuro's play was performed. But that somehow made her uneasy. And besides: she always dreamed of a perfect fiancé for Vera; she wanted to see her child in good hands and was convinced she'd have found an appealing, intelligent and rich husband if only "this" Andrijašević hadn't shown up on Wednesday. When there was talk of his inheritance, fine—but now?

Then again—this "non-engagement of an engagement" had gone on for far too long. Mrs. Nina thought, more than three years before, that within no more than two and a half years, Andrijašević would have come to take her daughter. After that, four years passed—and again, nothing. Now, what is this excuse for final exams? He could have finished everything already, and then talk of marriage would have been more appropriate. (Mrs. Hrabar did not consider that, for Vera's sake, Đuro had quit law school, where he had been enrolled for four semesters, and only switched to philosophy so that he could graduate sooner).

"Certainly—it is high time for a draconian measure. Let's assume the best possible outcome where he passes the exams. How will they live after that? And at the end of the day, we will, ultimately, still run the risk of him leaving *our* girl. In two or three years, Vera will be past the age when you can still count on suitors. What then?"

Mrs. Hrabar was alarmed to think that her daughter might be left unprovided for. She also knew that Vera could make a living by her talents, but this she considered true misfortune, a fate even worse than marrying Andrašijević.

The only thing she feared—her daughter's resolve. This is why she wanted to speak with her husband first, to muster enough courage to tell Vera. If one could distract the girl, even a little, from Andrijašević, the rest—Mrs. Nina thought—would follow on its own.

She remembered all the gentlemen who had been interested in Vera the year before when, despite her daughter's opposition and the cold shoulder from Đuro's side, her mother managed to take her daughter to a few parties.

*

Vera took Đuro's announcement quite calmly. Feelings for him had already taken hold of her; from their sudden young love affair that had completely shaken her four years before, she had developed a quiet and secure conviction of their future life together.

The men who came into contact with her before Andrijašević had all behaved similarly. Impeccably dressed, more or less witty in society, more or less talented for music. These men, like her, all lived in an atmosphere of level-headed etiquette; they always talked about theater, ice skating, travel and literature—with equal ease, the same smile, and the same calm gestures.

Andrijašević was obviously not from the same world; as a rule, he did not talk much, and if he noticed anything, he took his words far more seriously than the others. At first, Vera was not altogether at ease with his method of communication. Still, after the conversation about Tolstoy, which was eternally etched on her mind, she knew that Andrijašević's behavior was coming from the depths of his soul, that it was the result of hours of intellectual labor. But her maiden thoughts did not stop there; she immediately invented for him a legendary aura—his intelligence, which had attracted her from the first moment, now seemed the culmination of a life full of struggles and suffering. And immediately, as her feelings for him grew stronger, she thought of herself as a kind, compassionate sister or a sweet friend who wanted to comfort the tribulations of this strange and mysterious man.

The word 'love' didn't come to her mind, even less so any of the notions she had associated with falling in love: dancing, visiting family, getting engaged, and so forth. She interpreted her feelings as affection. Her awareness of the many literary descriptions of relationships between witty women and brilliant husbands gave her acquaintance with Andrijašević, an intelligent man and a writer, the aura of a halo.

When Andrijašević did not try to contact her for several days after the discussion about Tolstoy and failed to apologize for not coming to a party, Vera felt this "affection" was powerful. She began to think more about him and interpret his absences by imagining that Andrijašević also had a great liking for her but that he strove to suppress this inclination. She could not divine the reason for this and started to blame herself, inventing all possible reasons for his being "mad" at her—yet not finding a good one.

Đuro's poem, his transparent and painful confession of love, had a tempestuous impact on her. A hundred emotions seethed in her bosom—and finally, they all came together as an enormous amount of compassion for him, which drove her to sign the letter with her first initial.

But as the time of the meeting neared, Vera lost her audacity. Ultimately, she started to blame herself for her poor strategy and for writing to him. She decided to act unfriendly around him—but she dropped all these intentions when she realized Andrijašević loved her. She did not even need the letter from him that was delivered by mail the next day. Throughout the night, Vera did not close her eyes, blaming her behavior, recalling the contorted, tortured grimace on Andrijašević's face and his desperate words in parting. At that moment, he also revealed the deception of her notions of "affection" and "friendship" towards Đuro—and after the tears and prayers of that night, Vera woke up to the new realization that her life was increasingly tied to Andrijašević's. She no longer saw anything strange in hiding his letter from her mother, who by chance was not at home when the mail man brought it. In the afternoon, relatively calm, convinced of the necessity of all she was doing, she sent her confession to Andrijašević.

*

Those first days were, for her love, the most turbulent. Afterward, the way she communicated with Đuro on the outside changed very little; they knew that they loved each other and lived in happiness, satisfied with their meetings during Đuro's visits, a warm handshake, and a quiet understanding, when listening to the conversations between their peers, about music and everything else that had filled their lives before their relationship. Only rarely were they able to converse for a longer time; Andrijašević never asked her for extended encounters or anything that might seem alarmingly inappropriate. Until Đuro returned to Vienna, no one knew of their love; they never spoke to each other in front of others using intimate address. Đuro was allowed to ask Vera out for the first time only after everything was revealed to his mother, and there, on the very day of his departure, their lips pressed together in a kiss for the first time.

Later, after lengthy correspondence, they learned all about each other. Đuro sent Vera letters spanning multiple pages, with impressions, feelings, and memories; and Vera—far more restrained in manifesting her feelings—recited the simple events of her life, which at all times were full of love for him. She learned to seek his advice related to any issue, to give him family news, describe new acquaintances;—and their love grew more and more in their correspondence, giving their relationship a mature and serious seal.

Her mother was, at the very least, pleased that this commitment was a secret from the world; she had no idea that Đuro and Vera, with their letters, were laying the groundwork for a peaceful future life. Vera became more serious, stopped showing interest in parties and girlfriends—and several times, Mrs. Nina—afraid of her own words—found the opportunity to chide her, telling her she was behaving like an 'old maid.'

But honestly, her love for Andrijašević had turned into a sense of duty. Strictly brought up, she found the most beautiful side of love precisely in her decision to be faithful, to help her husband as a companion for life.

Over time her feeling became unmovable support; the pleasure of actually touching a man was extraneous to Vera, and the longer the engagement lasted, the more calm and realistic she saw her future life.

The girl did not understand that the main reason for her inner peace was growing ever more distant from the girlish bloom of young age. Mrs. Nina, more than anyone, felt this too: she was dissatisfied after watching Vera develop the habits of a lady who was no longer young. Her female friends were marrying, and Vera no longer understood her more youthful friends. With her mother, she became increasingly interested in housekeeping, became very private about her personal hygiene, read serious books, and started conversing with older people. A year before, when Đuro wrote to her that a woman should enter into marriage with devotion and merit as men do, she collected a pile of books and passed the qualifying exam to become a teacher. Nina Hrabar, who was also not getting any younger, was tortured by Vera's drift away from the future her mother wanted for her only daughter. To see her as a happy young woman, married to a husband who could at least maintain the lifestyle she currently enjoyed. Vera was moving toward accepting a future life with fewer means than her present ones and this took her farther from her mother's understanding of what constituted a successful life. And so, lately (especially since Đuro had to go to Vienna because "his studies, which give back nothing tangible anyway" had not yet been completed), mutual misunderstandings were more frequent. Vera, who used to confide everything in her mother, provoked a rift between mother and daughter by being so steadfastly on the side of her fiancé in all conversations about Andrijašević. Days of awkward silence and unspoken distance followed—and Mr. Hrabar himself often felt that things in his family were not as good and cheerful as before.

*

Mrs. Nina decided this time she would not give up and—in whichever way—she would free her daughter from the influence of Andrijašević, to whom, after his last announcement, she invariably referred as "your student" or "him." She was fearful for Vera—even more alarmed by the letters, especially the significant ones—so she thought that inviting Đuro to Zagreb to "seriously talk to him" would be best. She said nothing to Vera about the letter. Still, when Andrijašević announced his imminent arrival, she knew she had to inform her daughter.

In fear of this conversation, she delayed the announcement day after day; but since it was near the hour of Đuro's departure for Zagreb, she used the first opportunity to confess it to Vera.

"Mama! Why did you do this without my knowledge? I see no reason to hide it."

"Sorry, Vera, but you must believe that all I do is because I love you and am worried about your future. And this thing can't remain the way you want."

"Why not?"

"How nice. You're bound to this student, you stay away from society and go nowhere. And yet he has no obligations to you. He first said he would finish in three years, but then did nothing. Now he's still not finished. He had previously spoken of assets; now, there is not even a penny. In the end, he'll say he doesn't care for you; and you will become, my dear, should this situation persist and you are not provided for, you will become a great sorrow for my old age and your father's. Had you listened to me, all this would have been different..."

Her mother began to sob right there, first swallowing back her tears and then louder to instill a sense of guilt in her daughter. Vera didn't know what her mother wanted (who didn't dare say she wanted to break off the engagement), but her mother's tears hurt and finally, more to calm her than with serious intentions, she agreed to let her mother talk to Đuro and to 'make things right.'

"Just promise me you will not oppose my decisions."

"Whatever suits Đuro will suit me," answered Vera.

*

Three days later, in the evening, Andrijašević was sitting alone at a table at his hotel restaurant, thinking about his visit to the Hrabars.

"How seriously the old woman spoke—almost as if she were on stage. How cunningly she arranged things so I wouldn't remain alone with Vera for a moment! The old man even had to forego his card game; he was certainly not happy about that, but to no avail, he had to submit to taking part in our interesting discussions."

"I had to cower, catching only glimpses of the conversation. No matter what, I am never keen to be close to people. Being alone is a wonderful thing. Look, now I

can think over and study all that happened; that afternoon, they overwhelmed me with all their dramatic
spectacles, and I had not even a shadow of thought left
in my brain. They grilled me as if I were a high-school
student at an exam!"

Andrijašević likes the word 'dramatic spectacle,'
mostly because of the label, it seems to him—but only
for a moment—that the spectacle at Hrabar's was not so
very horrible.

This is what happened:

Vera and her father met him at the station. Immediately after they greeted him, she told him they hoped
he'd come to their house later and she whispered to him
that her mother was ready for a serious talk. Mr. Hrabar
had no idea how to behave with him; in the end, everyone was relieved when Đuro left for the hotel.

At the Hrabars, he met the parents; "Vera will come
later because she had to go somewhere." Mrs. Nina
complained to Đuro of a headache, asked him in half-
baked sentences about his stay in Slavonia, and jumped
right in to talk about her letter.

"I wrote to you because, as you will see for yourself, my
daughter's happiness must be in my heart. As parents, my
husband and I want to know exactly what's happening."

"Please, please!" (This bold outburst was for Đuro
quite daring; when Nina Hrabar continued, the thought
came to him: So what does she truly mean by 'what's
happening?')

"I don't think it's offensive," interceded old Hrabar,
"that we wish to be transparent with you. *Clara pacta,
boni amici.* We have so far had confidence in you ..."

"I hope I have done nothing to lower myself to your eyes."

"This thing has certainly become a little awkward for us." Mrs. Hrabar suddenly started to talk abruptly and sternly. "I believed that by this year, you would be in a position to fulfill your obligations to Vera."

"It is not my fault that this has not yet been possible."

"It certainly isn't our fault," said Mrs. Hrabar. "Vera is no longer a young lady, and we cannot let things go on like this."

After that, the turn came for the obvious and, to Andrijašević, familiar questions about his future existence. But this time, Vera's mother was not listening calmly to his explanations; she instead commented ironically on his possible career options. Đuro was utterly discouraged by this awkward situation, and in the end, he calmly listened to her parents' words, from which he understood more and more clearly how irrelevant he was to them. They came across as mediocre to him— terribly mediocre as they talked about his love as if it were something that could be erased like an item in a merchant's account. He felt neither pain nor anger—he only wanted to say goodbye as soon as possible and not have to listen to them.

Finally, Mrs. Nina made her request ("and is the least we can ask from you") that Đuro return to them only when he finished his exams and that he would not write to Vera.

"My daughter has effectively been compromised because of you. Everyone wonders why she doesn't attend parties. While you were still a student, I closed an eye;

but now I am telling you openly that it is not right that my daughter is being left behind because of you. You promised to finish your studies, and you only finished halfway," and here Mrs. Nina started to line up her objections again, paying scant attention to whether her words were avoiding any mention of Đuro's seriousness, maturity, and even honesty.

The torrent of the woman's words was interrupted by Mr. Hrabar, who did not find being rude at all appropriate.

"You are, Doctor, Sir, at an age when you certainly no longer need to be reminded of how serious and important are the obligations implicit in an engagement. You are not bound to our daughter by an official liaison, so even now it makes no sense to talk about it since you don't have a secure existence, nor could you provide one for Vera. On the other hand, our indulgence gave you some rights, primarily to correspond with Vera."

This reasoned exposition wounded Đuro far worse than Mrs. Hrabar's blatant hostility.

"Simply say what you want from me—it is entirely unnecessary to explain. You have the right to throw me out if you wish; I cannot listen to this much longer. You want me to refrain from corresponding with Vera ...? For how long? A year? Until I have finished the exam? And during that time, you will take her to balls, look for a husband, is that it?"

"Please don't use that tone," said Mr. Hrabar seriously. "No point in getting upset without reason. The matter is simple: we only want the correspondence between Vera and you to cease until you can come for her."

("Oh, if only I could get out of here! I'll tell them something crazy—I'll insult them! Anything, anything, so they don't bother me anymore, let me go!")

"Good. I must agree with all of this, and I agree with it all."

At that moment, Vera entered the room. Without hiding her satisfaction, the mother immediately told her daughter that they, her parents, had just settled with 'Mr. Andrijašević' on how to 'wait until the good Doctor comes for Vera.'

"And you agreed not to write to me at all?"

Vera used the informal '*ti*' for the first time in front of her father and mother.

Andrijašević was utterly shaken by this.

He looked at her—and her two eyes met his, full of restrained tears.

"I had to agree, Vera. I have no right to you other than what has been given to me."

"Please, please, we respect your feelings, but it's still better this way," said Mr. Hrabar.

Vera stood at the door, not taking off her fur coat.

"Đuro, how long will this take?"

"A few months..."

Đuro's words crossed his lips with effort; all he was hearing and saying was foreign to him.

"You see, Vera, now everything depends on the good Doctor's will." Mr. Hrabar broke the awkward silence that arose after Andrijašević's words.

Vera still hadn't looked at him. The mother was obviously afraid of an emotional outburst and did not want to participate in this exchange.

But the daughter neither cried nor complained. She ambled over to Đuro, stood beside him as if to mark her place in the house, and said more to her mother than to the one concerned by her words:

"When you agree, you know I won't resist. Mama is afraid of the world. Let her be. You know me and I know you and we won't change over these few months. You promised not to write. So be it. You and I will keep this promise. But then, once this short time passes, only we, you and I, will decide."

("Ah, you're talking about a short time—but it will be quite long! And what is this whole request other than a comedy! If only they would leave and I could speak with you in private—to complain!" thought Đuro to himself.)

Vera's determination confused her mother, who felt that the effect of Vera's words should be ignored (Mr. Hrabar looked at his 'little girl' in complete astonishment) and began to say that, of course, 'the good Doctor' should not be surprised if she took Vera to social events, and so forth.

Andrijašević could clearly see: I am not wanted. They don't need me; they are getting rid of me. And when Vera started answering her mother and Mrs. Hrabar switched to her previous sharp tone, talking about the 'uncertain future'—every word began physically to hurt Đuro. Everything seemed funny to him at times—both Vera's sobs and her father's consolations. He had to listen to Vera's rebuke and Mrs. Hrabar's answers—and for the first time, he fully and clearly understood that Vera's mother could barely tolerate him, that she had been preparing for this conclusion for a long time. He was somehow ashamed that he had to hear these family quarrels and the enumeration of his own mistakes with which Mrs. Hrabar responded to Vera's reproach. The more Vera emphasized her faith in him, the more helpless and miserable he felt.

"Escape, escape!" was his only thought. And when Vera finally fell into the armchair and began to choke on her tears, he could barely muster the strength to stroke her hair, to tell her that he would come soon, that this matter would not end this way.

Out on the street, he took a deep breath and slowly, at first without thinking, headed for a café. As if someone had rescued him from an accursed dance, he forgot at first what had just happened. He ran into a couple of acquaintances and started talking about this and that, but when the lamps in the café and outside in the dusk of the winter evening were lit, and people began to move like shadows on the sidewalk, he felt a restlessness and the need to be alone.

He found a tavern with only a few customers and sat there for two hours in a corner by the pillar, reliving the scene at the Hrabars' for the one-hundredth time.

*

This all ended in an unspeakably nasty way! Four years of life, hope, peace—they think to blow all that away with a ridiculous conversation about means of support ... Is it even possible to tear asunder a relationship that bound two people without all the official ties but with ties more potent than a blood relation? Love, dreams, the future—it's all nothing. I guess they have found a fat *bonhomme* of the seventh income class for Vera—and now they can't imagine that someone can live without a large pension.

"Taken care of"—how many times did they say that this afternoon! For the sake of that care, everything between us should be forgotten ... If only death had come—illness—earthquake—if at least something completely unexpected had occurred. If Vera had fallen in love with another fellow—that would be fine; I would have gritted my teeth and then gone quietly. But like this! Requiring me to move away just because it takes two to three years before you get to the point when every day you can have a dessert after lunch...

"Yes, to move away... They want it. The old lady said so openly. Everything else is an excuse: the condition that I must not write to her and Mr. Hrabar's consolation that he hopes to see me as a tenured professor in two years' time is all a lie. They want to take her from me, humiliate me, and push me into a corner."

Andrijašević's feelings changed suddenly and without reason. For a moment, he was appalled by how the Hrabars treated his and Vera's love; but then, again, he began to ironize about his destiny and hopes.

"This is an old song. *Born without luck* ... What was the point of moving from Vienna? Why come to Zagreb, find her, and wake up to a new life? By today I could have finished school a long, long time ago. I could be some kind of lawyer's clerk who drinks his allotted amount every day and waits for death. Why then all this effort and torment?"

"And all because of one fatal bit of nonsense: Toma's death. Had Toma not died, I would have stayed up there for another semester and finished the exams ... Calm down, calm down, you fool! Everything is written in the stars, as the Eastern folks who before us asked the sphinx about life say... It makes no sense to me to think that everything could be different! Of course, I could win the lottery; what a foolish thought ... "

At times, all this seemed ludicrous. The disproportion between the ties linking him to Vera and the trivial question about a supplementary income appeared so huge that the whole event became comical. The waiter from his corner glanced over strangely two or three times (the inn was almost completely empty) at this stranger who sneered from time to time.

"First contact with that so-called life—and here it is: tears, humiliation, bitterness. Poor Vera—she must be suffering ... what they must have told her over these few last days! ... And now?"

"Go home—get lost in a small place and study ... How will you find the strength to endure a year of effort and tiresome endeavor? You mustn't write to her—they came up with a wonderful condition..."

The servant brought, without waiting for orders, yet another full glass.

"Ah. That's the only truth you can get your hands on ... *In vino veritas*... Maniacs think this means that drunk people tell the truth ... Wine is the truth; that's the whole point ... Yes, alcohol intoxicates you, it anesthetizes, it masters everything. Nothing can resist it. It needs no fantasies or feelings—it turns you into someone else; it takes you away from the ugly present...."

With the pleasure of alcohol, his irony grew. Andrijašević found all his work in recent years more and more meaningless; staring into the smoke of a cigarette, into a stupor, looking at himself as some poor beggar who was so mad that he hoped to find mercy in good people.

"A beggar, a beggar ... a fool who believed life could be tolerable... And now you are at the door ... travel on, you wretched soul until the night swallows you ..."

Ultimately, he was filled with rage—desperate, bloody anger at himself, his gullibility, and all his foolish dreams. He seemed to be weeping from rage—not with his eyes, but as if somewhere deep inside, sob after sob, something was breaking and hurting and burning ...

"Lenau's verse... how he sang to the three gypsies: *wie man's verspielt, vergeigt und vertrinkt und es dreimal verachtet* ... Everyone should be playful, sleep on it, get drunk, scratch it away three times...."

After a long time, Andrijašević, having drunk himself into a stupor, found himself in the company of women whom he could not look at without disgust after his first meeting with Vera.

In the morning, he traveled to Rijeka to his mother on the first train.

*

He remained lethargic and bored for two months. The reply to his job petition was not forthcoming; as the beginning of the second half of the school year approached, Andrijašević thought there might be no vacancies for him.

"And that would be perfectly in line with my misfortunes."

On the last day of January, he received a telegram that he had been appointed a junior instructor in Senj. The news cheered him, but he immediately remembered that he must not tell Vera ("She can only find out about my appointment from the newspapers!"), and, without enthusiasm, he prepared for his new residence.

Chapter IV

I was going through my papers today—and here's what I found: notes from Zdenci. I read them—so now it is clear to me that in those few impressions, I recorded my *état d'âme*. It seems as if on paper I'd affixed my photograph, captured at one particular moment.

Well—let's move on! My desire to write may ebb again and stop, but in a month or so I will know where I was on my journey at that time.

A lot has changed since I last wrote in Zdenci about my decision to respond to the invitation and travel to Zagreb. So, so much...

That night does not give me peace. To get drunk—and end up in that kind of company... no, I have no remorse because I know we don't do anything of our own free will, yet still, it hurts.

I remember one evening in Vienna when I was listening to Beethoven's Pastoral Symphony. How many times had Vera and I played it! At the concert, among strangers, it was as if she were somewhere near me—the sounds not only reached my ears but echoed in my heart. It was as if Vera were somewhere in the hall—hiding in a box, invisible to the crowd—I felt her closeness: even more— I could feel how every note would sound to her ...

And she wrote to me a few days later that that same evening she was distraught and remembered our playing music together.

Dream? Imagination?

I do not know. *Ignoramus*. But it seemed ridiculous to repress a beautiful truth by discussing the materiality of spiritual functions. What do I care what a brain cell thinks or if it is a higher, intangible bearer of our spirituality. What do I care if some invisible membrane flickered and carried a wave of that feeling or if some supernatural power simultaneously played on the harp our 'ego'—! That instrument, whatever its name, whether made of blood or nothing—I used it to leap hundreds of kilometers and knock on her door, the door to her soul.

And what if Vera had felt my rage, my self-destructive despair that night ...

Ah, if I only could write to her!

I am increasingly tempted to break my promise. It wouldn't be difficult: you write a letter, send it, and entrust everything to faith. If Vera is home alone, she will receive it.

And if she doesn't?

Ah, no—that would be ugly. Mr. Hrabar would rebuke me for not keeping my word. And I would humiliate myself in Vera's eyes.

I know well that she wouldn't do anything behind her mother's back, especially now. Well—I must not destroy her faith in me; I must not show myself weak.

Fugue

We will endure.

*

February the 8th

Toša was right when he chastised us writers for describing only weaklings. Even worse: we not only describe them, we *are* weaklings. We are people of caprice and of moment without resilience.

Now that I remember my last stay in Zagreb, I feel almost ashamed. Why had I, in a second, lost all my strength? First of all—I should have anticipated that I would now have to think very seriously about a future for Vera and me—and give an account of this to her parents. But then—was it necessary to submit to them immediately, allow them to lecture me, and then agree to everything Mrs. Hrabar demanded?

It was my first battle—and I laid down my weapons. Not a good sign.

How I cursed the old lady in my mind for that evening! And I hated her—poor thing. And yet—she was not entirely wrong. The only unpleasant thing about her is that she doesn't trust me. By the way, what does she want? Either I take Vera soon, or she'll find another husband for her. She is old, so she may be afraid of death; she is afraid to leave her daughter without security, hence her simple logic.

Had I been more assertive, I could have easily proved to her that we would not split up just because I was not allowed to write to Vera and that she will wait another year.

Why a year? I could take the exam as early as this summer. I must grab the books right away.

February the 11th

I have not managed to adjust to the multitude of new feelings. New people—a new life, a school, and a small town—it's a lot all at once.

Most of all, I was impressed by the nature. Nature is weird here—weird and scary.

There is the bura, a gale wind that blows in Rijeka as well; it grows strong, smashes and destroys. How many times have we, as students, chain-linked our arms and run to be swept along by the gusts of wind!

But Rijeka is a city with a harbor, cafés, trams, car noise, and all sorts of people. One doesn't feel the bura there as one does here: people are busy, in a hurry, hastening along the street, ducking into public places and huddling in groups. In Rijeka, the bura is an unpleasant obstacle to traffic, much like rain or an excessive chill in the air.

Here the bura is another matter altogether—it is a living force that blows in like a sort of supernatural dragon. People in a small town don't work as much and don't live as fast a life. Here, there are no nervous entertainments at the time of day set aside for lunch or dinner as there are in the metropolis. Here people live more like herbs—which is why they are more affected by nature.

The bura comes—and here it blows harder—and half of the people do not dare to venture forth; why fight the elements when your purpose is to go for a walk, not to run to a remote office or a boat? You lock yourself in the house and close the door tight. The few who must be outdoors quickly take the shortest way home. Only those who have nowhere else to eat stay at the inn. And the storm howls, howls, and roars, through the empty streets. Even the heaviest precipitation from a few hours earlier dries up instantly. It moves like a massive spur with a hundred spikes, peeking around every corner, whistling in every crook and cranny. Who wants to face it?

And it moves further out to sea; it blows irregularly now in gusts, it does not make big waves but mows. The trace of its touch shows on the sea, and it flies with terrible speed. It appears to slide over the sea surface. And across the water, on the island, where it crashes into caves—the bura raises vortices of foam.

It is not like a conflagration; it does not kill, it destroys no one who fears it. It is not like a flood because it does not swallow without mercy.

The bura is something higher and more beautiful. It slaps you on the cheeks, presses against your shoulder, chokes your breath, and doesn't let you move forward. Fight it!—that is what its whistling is telling you. Step by step you must wrest from it your right until it releases you to proceed on down the street. And it is almost never so furious that it does not respect your strength and courage: resist it and you will make it through to the end.

Just don't run from it! If you turn around and try to run, you are immediately mocked. You—you want to compete in speed with it, the bura, that runs faster than the wildest locomotive! Don't even try!—It lifts you like a feather into the air and flings you against the wall.

Braving the bura is only for the strong and the brave, not for the wise or the careful. There is nothing a fire engine or boat can do against it—it still rules its surroundings, free as a wild animal in a primeval forest.

And it is not ugly, it does not blow in with fog or dark clouds: the sky is clear when it blows, and the brighter it is, the happier it celebrates its feast.

My blood flows more vigorously when I feel it. It is vast and proud; never disrespectful towards us. It only keeps some corners for itself, corners you cannot visit.

There is a proverb that the bura is born in Senj. It seems to me that here it is in its youth, with its primal force.

*

February the 14th

School is much more pleasant than I expected. However, my teaching duties are connected to all the boring and superfluous things (a philosopher with a whip! Beautiful picture); overall, everything is agreeable.

Observing the students is interesting. Luckily, they didn't ask me to teach the lowest grades because of the classes I instruct, so I don't have to deal with children who can't even blow their noses. Fourth-graders are already surprisingly mature. I do not know whether this is an exception among the local children, but there are a few natural talents here—the boys don't shy away from my questions. And most surprising to me, the subject itself interests them.

It's a little more challenging in the higher grades. In the seventh, I have to torture them with actual calculus, but they haven't even mastered the basics of algebra. I am most comfortable in the eighth. There are two young men who will make something of themselves. Pedagogical wisdom may gainsay this, but when I speak I pay the most attention to them and leave the others more or less alone. Indeed—they understand me, and they even understand psychology with no difficulty.

I would like to know what first impression I have left on my students. I notice one thing: I am too nicely dressed compared to my colleagues. In a small town, people pay little attention to their appearance. It seems that students are not used to seeing teachers whose white shirts are as white as mine. But, I did notice that the other day, when I came to school dressed casually, my colleague Žuvić greeted me with a hint of malice.

Have the students given me a nickname because of that?

One thing is terrible here: they don't call anyone by name. I can't remember the countless nicknames I've heard these last few days. The inn where I eat is Pod Nehajem, Palčić is the proprietor—but that's not what they call the inn or him. Referring to the inn, they say, 'Under the Archway,' and him—God knows why—they call him 'Elder,' though he is young.

One thing makes me especially happy: I have found a lovely apartment. Here it's not like in Vienna, where you need a room just to sleep (I recall that there were plenty of us who never needed lamps but only had a candle for that couple of hours while you undress and lie down); here, I will get used to sitting at home. And I have a view of the vast, beautiful sea, and the island across the water, naked and rugged, magnificent.

In the first few days, I have a lot to do. They loaded me up with catalogs, statistics, and papers—all to be filled out by me. But I'll get rid of that soon, so I'll have more time to work in the lab. I have done nothing concrete for several months, so this pleases me.

Altogether, not at all bad. But I am writing too much—and today (I firmly decided to do so), I must prepare a letter for the dean's office in Vienna asking him how to receive a transcript of my dissertation.

*

February the 15th

I read today what I wrote yesterday in this diary of mine. Look!—I have somehow acquired the skill of recording life's trivia.

Good sign! When I don't philosophize, I feel fresher and more ready for work.

My job interests me far more than I previously thought.

So far, my interest in physics has always been quite abstract. While studying for the exam, I managed to delve into calculations and demonstrations—so profoundly that I would forget about the passage of time. It often happened that, in my thoughts, I would fly far away from these seemingly dry numbers—all the way to the border where the natural sciences meet philosophy.

In reality, every beginner who has become superficially acquainted with a certain branch of knowledge is happy to dream of ramifications that neither this nor any other knowledge can have. When I first started studying chemistry—nobody could force me to look and pay attention to the details and the simplest properties of the elements! I immediately flew past this and was ready to think about the fundamental theoretical axioms of chemistry from an ostensibly higher point of view.

A dreamer remains a dreamer!

And yet—one can acquire science only slowly and with effort. Only then, when you understand the torturous alphabet of the basic concepts, can you allow yourself to ponder on the laws of nature. You must first go through all the simple experiments, learn almost by heart the robust material of human observations—and then you mature, you can bring some order to all that, see the constants by which natural transformations take place.

Now I'm going in a completely different direction. I must explain to the students how to derive a physical law from an experiment. I have to identify with their thought process and explain everything to them as clearly as possible.

This makes me happy. Especially when I see improvement. And I, who believed that God created me to be anything but a scholar, am quite pleased when I succeed at demonstrating that a stone and a feather fall at the same time from a certain height.

I only notice that one must be well prepared for such an explanation. Knowledge and school teaching are two entirely different things; someone—if I remember correctly—said that pedagogy is an art.

It takes a lot of my time. During these fifteen days, I barely managed to review anything for myself.

*

February the 17th

I can't remember at this moment if, in literature, there are any specific books about teachers. There are many jokes about them forgetting umbrellas—the teacher somehow became a fellow much like a lieutenant.

But I do not agree. It seems to me that looking at teachers would be especially worthwhile. They are a crew of interesting and profound individuals.

Of my colleagues, a good half are worthy of observation. It's true, the other half are nothing—but I guess that's the way with every profession. The other half could just as well be merchants, judges or priests. They would fit in anywhere, as they do here—nobodies, people identified by a number.

Well I never!—what a lovely expression: people identified by a number. Convicts are numbered, and other than that, they are all dressed the same way and have their hair clipped in the same way. People like these have much in common with convicts—taken as individuals, they don't mean a thing; they become relevant only as a crowd because they can shout. This is neither due to vocation or schooling; as some may think, there must be people like them, everywhere lacking in intelligence.

I am most interested in Lukačevski. An odd fellow. He is in the first department, i.e., among the exceptional ones, and certainly holds first place among them. Tall, strong, but lean. There is something very stern in his expression, and his eyes are completely dead—gray. If he didn't have an English beard, he would look entirely like an ascetic friar.

I liked Lukačevski right away: first because of his name (I love Polish people very much; his father was Polish, a doctor somewhere in the coastal region), and then because of the absolute coldness with which he greeted me. The others were all more or less kind to me as you are expected to be with a guest (ah, the first day!), and two or three colleagues flattered me for my novels. He just bowed and said calmly:

"From Vienna, I see—hmm, too big of a jump."

I later learned that the man had exquisite manners; he must have come from a good family. It bothers me that he's dressed somehow—I don't even know how to say it: his outfit is clean, it fits him well—but it looks as if he's been wearing it for three or four years. He reminded me of an equestrian wearing attire in lifeless colors, while the others all wore yellow and red.

Now I dine with him at the inn. He doesn't say much but—it seems—reads more than anyone else. I was surprised at how well he knows Vienna. The other day we talked about theater and entertainment; he asked me about this and that; I didn't even know how to answer his detailed questions. It feels as if he could have arrived from Vienna only a month ago. I mentioned that some of these halls and amusement spots could not yet have been open when he was at the university (he is over thirty-five), and I asked him if he had recently visited Vienna.

"No," he said shortly, turning the conversation to another subject.

For now, I will not make enquires about him; I definitely need to discover his story.

*

The 20th

Ugh, today is nasty. It's raining—the sky is heavy and a revolting green. Today, the sea looks muddy—a torrent is pouring into it, so the water is as red as clay up to half of the harbor.

I'm nervous. The southern wind always takes a toll on my nerves. I feel forsaken—I am alone ...

Vera, Vera, where are you now? It is three o'clock in the afternoon—you must be sitting at the piano...

And I have had to give up the piano; I have no instrument, and I don't know anyone who owns one.

This state of mind mustn't go on too long. I wouldn't survive it—I'd have to run away.

And—where to? I can't go to Vera...

*

The 24th

The southerly wind lasted three days. I shall go crazy if this type of weather is a common occurrence here. I cannot work, I can think of nothing to do. I tried to have fun in the lab—but the humidity bothers me and there was only dim light. I was so restless that it didn't help me to start writing the catalog I need to finish once and for all. This is impossible! You start, write three names, and stare around the dim room. You run outside.

But where? In weather like this, life in a small town must be awful. There is no alternative but to the local watering hole.

So for three days, I spent almost all my free time there. At least there are lights and people...

And, for God's sake, what kind of people! Is it possible that they honestly live their lives like this? I did not get to know them when I went there only for lunch and dinner. But over these three days—these folks did not move from their tables. The office and the inn—of course only until 8 in the evening; then comes the turn for family and sleep. And you know what they do? They play a terribly dull card game. In the afternoon, from one to three, in the evening, from five to eight or nine. Today, tomorrow, the day after—every day. Can they not hear themselves? In three days, I have learned everything: their nicknames, their jokes, what a retired elementary school supervisor might say, how angry one of them is and how loud another shouts.

And they are not bored. They cannot wait to meet. Every day—forever.

This is called—living!

These people are not evil, they are not disgusting. But they are empty, completely empty. You know one, and you know them all. They have almost identical habits. They even drink the same number of glasses of beer.

Yes—I once lived like that, dead, with no feelings, monotonously, tediously. In Vienna for the second year, I, too, needed a certain number of glasses every day. But this resulted from mental weariness, spent nerves after a crisis.

And all these people, after all, are entirely ordinary, it seems indeed, that they are not even dissatisfied.

Oh God, oh God—is it possible that I will have to live like this?

Ah, that's crazy—I guess I won't be staying here forever—there are larger towns here.

*

February the 26th

Lukačevski does not play cards and, he does not seem very friendly with the locals. He stands aside, watching the others. But he, too, drinks, indeed more than others.

Strange—I noticed he, too, was awfully nervous in those days of southerly wind. I even asked him why.

"The weather, Sir."

I told him this weather also had a negative effect on me.

"You'll get used to everything. Man is worse than an animal because man believes he has free will and thus forces himself to get used to things. You will have a lot to swallow, my young friend."

He is not much older than me, so I reprimanded him for how he speaks to me, in an "I'm older than you," protective tone.

"You are still young, young—know why? Don't be angry if I tell you that you still belong to yourself. You have not yet arrived at the point of being assimilated.

Look at their card games—the players all look alike. That's true for the thirty- and the fifty-year-olds. Age has nothing to do with it—you will remain young until this provincial life catches you in its daily grind."

"And you stand aside and are not a part of it?" I said timidly.

He frowned immediately.

"I don't like to talk about myself. But do you think that by now I wish to move away from my corner where I've been sitting for five years? Well, I do not."

After this conversation, we drank more than usual; Lukačevski, who otherwise never speaks about work, began to give me advice.

"Maybe I'll spoil an illusion of yours," he told me. "But you're an intelligent man, so you don't need such things. Listen to me: I overheard some conversations—you will learn whose in the fullness of time—I listened to some conversations and realized that there are resentments because of your innovative teaching style in the more advanced classes. Students may rise up against it. And why do you need this? Don't get carried away! Only work as much as is adequate; do as little as they require to keep you on. You still don't know how beastly a student can become." (It's not nice of him to dislike young people. It seems to me that he hates both the school and the kids.)

What do you mean that I teach too smartly? Perhaps they don't understand?

Lukačevski is mistaken—the children seem to love me. And why would anyone mind how I organize my classes?

March the 5th

I cannot go on like this. I notice that I am hardly doing anything. The school takes up so much of my time—besides, with our resources, it's impossible to show anything to the pupils. I have to struggle to patch up the most crucial experiments.

I've been here for over a month and have given no serious thought to regular studying!

I will have to force myself to arrange some sort of schedule for each day.

Ah, if they only had a café here! It seems to me that things would be much better. I could sit in the café for the time I needed to rest, and then I would take care of everything.

As it is, they drag me into a tavern—I can't stay all day at home or at school. I always stay at the tavern until dinner, so I never find a way out of my laziness.

From tomorrow on, I will change. How will I, old donkey, learn to stick to the clock as students do?

Regardless—I must study for at least two hours a day.

*

The 8th

The only happy people on earth are those with a one-track mind. They are not affected by events, what the Romans called *vicissitudines vitae*.

We mock mathematicians for being so absorbed in their numbers, for living innocently without seeing what is going on around them. And yet this is arguably the most attractive formula for a good life.

You crawl into your room, to your books—and this is a world by itself. You are alone, and no one bothers you, you don't have to give account to anyone, and no one can take anything away from you.

In such a small town, this is the only alternative for survival. Living for something abstract that has nothing to do with all those boring and superfluous little things that merely fill the day but can't fill tedium.

But this is not in my nature. It must be that my father was a restless spirit—a wanderer around the world.

So what thing is there to fully occupy and sweep me up me so I can endure all the emptiness of life?

Literature?

Indeed, I haven't written anything for the longest time. But that wouldn't keep me busy for long either. It's difficult to believe in the value of what you yourself are creating. Working for others?—I am no altruist.

... What have I written now? I reread it right now—and I kind of like it.

I should be thinking about something altogether different: my obligations. In a year, I will have a great deal of work to do for the exam. And Vera is waiting...

I do not want to be alone. My thoughts assail me...

*

The 10th

My salary does not allow for any entertainment. As a student, I lived quite nicely in Vienna with the same income that does not suffice here. I already borrowed a hundred forints from my mother—and I am not comfortable writing to her again. Poor old woman, it is high time to stop eternally feeding other people's children and worrying about the welfare of others. The inheritance left by Uncle Toma is negligible, but for my mom, twenty forints a month is a lot of money.

I rob her of this, no doubt. But only for this year, we will take her to live with us.

Look—she has never met Vera, nor does she know anything about her. How distant I have become from my mother over the last few years!

Nevertheless, I still have to write to her to send me more money; I don't know whom to ask here. I am not so intimate yet with my colleagues; I routinely meet only with Lukačevski. And I'm not going to ask him.

Finally, it would be difficult to ask colleagues for even a little. How can Radović live on his salary with his wife and four children? However—he does not spend anything on himself except that he drinks (and sometimes gets from others) two glasses of beer daily. Now I understand why they fought so hard at the beginning of the semester to teach optional subjects. Those two hundred crowns must have been a real godsend for Radović.

He always looks dissatisfied anyway. I don't feel comfortable when I meet him on the street; he has a winter coat already entirely green from age.

*

March the 16th

I got drunk last night—and I have been hungover all day.

It's crazy that I couldn't make it to school. And it was Žuvić of all people whom I had to encounter after midnight.

Who knows what time it was? Lukačevski is the guilty one. There is something evil and cold in this man that I, nevertheless, find attractive. It is the consequence of my old obsession with performing psychological evaluations and seeing tragic conflicts everywhere.

Yet, who could say this cold and calm man must be truly desperate? Desperate to the end—so desperate, he no longer cares what happens to him.

I don't even know how we were left alone last night. Ah, yes, I remember now—I went for a walk in the afternoon along the road to Rijeka. The day is typical for midsummer; when the bura is not blowing and there is no rain, we feel as if we are in Nice. Mid-March—and today was already an actual summer day. The sea is calm, wide, sharp blue, as if fake. If Segantini had painted the sea, he would have caught its blueness. I was in a good mood—I walked fast, thought a lot, looked at the telegraph poles along the road, and remembered Vera.

When I got home, it was too claustrophobic in my room. I couldn't stand it—I thought it was a crime not to enjoy the beautiful day to its end.

I went, of course, to the tavern. There were many colleagues, and everyone was happy today. We simply drank too much—so I didn't feel like going home when the others left. (Where was Žuvić going when I met him much later?)

Lukačevski also kept me from leaving—and I stayed with him. All evening he didn't show that he was in a good mood—only when alone with me did he start laughing and joking.

"See how beautiful it is on such a fine day. People are nicer. See how kind and cheerful everyone was tonight. Poor people—tomorrow they will forget everything: Žuvić will again whisper to the headmaster that you are more a writer than a teacher, Radović will invest all his wisdom in correcting tasks that make no sense—in short, everything will revert to normal. Come out, brother, out of your skin! It's late."

I objected that he mostly sees the evil side of people. He laughed and defended himself:

"No, my friend, you'll see what animals people are." Animal and beast—those two words he especially loved. "I like you because you have not yet been forced by profession or life into such nests. But the others—my God!—they all know that whatever they do is worthless, of no benefit to them or anyone else, and yet they believe they are important—and they will recount the stupidest school affair as if it were God knows what."

"It's not like that, for God's sake! For example, the upbringing of children is where you can easily find something noble. Do you actually hold it against them if this man or that truly interpreted his vocation that way?"

"Please, what vocation! Žuvić became a professor because they gave him a scholarship; the other one because he himself had no idea what subject to pursue at university—and so on. There is no vocation here, as you call it. And what, please, prompted you to take this job?"

I, of course, did not want to tell him anything about the fact that I had abandoned the study of law for Vera's sake; instead, I started talking about how I liked my subject and schooling in general. This is, apparently, taboo for him; he hates it when someone says good things about the school.

"It will go away with time, my dear. It is fun while it lasts—I, too, was like that. But what will you do—there is no change; today, tomorrow—always lecturing and teaching the same, bother with that same brats—who can stand this over a long time? And outside of school—what to do in a small town? The French are clever people; they work until five or six o'clock, then dress in salon attire—and live for fun. They are looking for a change, trying to get something out of life for themselves. Meanwhile, what are we doing here?—You finish school and come to the tavern, and there you run into everyone else who also finished work. There is no change, joy, or energy in all this; it is mechanical."

"Well, you change; you've been here long, so look for other company."

"Who? Me?—Where should I go? I don't like the company of women, and men are all the same."

"Do something, anything, there are so many sports and amusements."

"Yes, I tried that. I'll show you at some point: I paint. But that's not enough. Everything should change; it does not help if you insist on wanting something. I don't belong—that's all. And neither do you, my friend. Life will force you as much as it has me—and you will obey, but you will not get used to it."

We spoke louder and louder and even argued. There was no one at the inn, only a napping waitress who served us our beers. Lukačevski was all inflamed and eager to prove to me that vocation and life in our region are worth nothing.

"There's no choice but to admit it's pathetic, my friend. Tell yourself: how have you lived so far? Maybe you ran out of luck, but you were in Vienna. You ate at a beer garden, and after that you went to a coffee shop, read newspapers from all over the world, sat next to beautiful women, and watched new people. Perhaps you also went to the theater—but even if you didn't, the city is a city. Ah, let the doctors know how foolish their praise of fresh air in the countryside is! I would rather spend an afternoon saturated in smoke than a hundred days like today. We are not, my friend, fit for this any longer! You know, I read the news every day, and I follow all the Viennese events. I know what is being offered today at the Burg and the exhibits at Miethke. So how are you going to get along with people who like it here—or even if they don't like it, they never knew how much better it could be."

"Well, it sounds like you're looking for a transfer!" I told him.

"Ah, please, where? You'd run from bad to worse. At least the sea is close by; I have made my peace with this as much as possible, and people are used to me—they leave me alone. And to come to a bigger city—what do I get out of it when nowhere do they give you enough salary to live on?"

"Still—to be so lonely..."

"Yes, it would be nicer to sit in a palace and talk to people in white shirts and ladies who do not have to cook. But there is no such thing. You will see for your-self; we who do not belong to this *milieu* must not even mix with it. Stay aside and be content that you have enough to eat, drink, and smoke and that you needn't humiliate yourself by begging one of them to lend you money."

"You are a terrible egoist."

"Today, my young man, getting excited about any-thing else is not fashionable. And it can't be done. Just try—they'll press you up against the wall and punch your snout so you'll never open your mouth again."

We became more and more melancholic. The wait-ress got up and lazily hung around us as the lights dimmed. She removed the tablecloths—and everything seemed sad, out of order. Eventually, we talked about marriage. I told Lukačevski that he would not last long living alone like this.

"Get married, right? Do you mean what you say? Do you know that the authorities really ought to ban all of us from marrying! It is the worst. Young people fall in love and marry, then come the worries and privation—hunger ensues, my dear. Because you are never satisfied, you become timid and clumsy, become afraid of the di-rector and the headmaster. You borrow from colleagues, from your savings, from a student's father. Anxiety about tomorrow kills you. If you aspire to doing some-thing, to doing it as well as possible, you can't. Day after day, dissatisfaction gnaws at your heart, you become grumpy and weak; you hate your wife and yourself. You finally settle down—you live in nirvana, and you will never again dig yourself out of debt, never experience another good meal. Eventually, you just start figuring out how to fill your two or three free hours—and then you come here and play ten or twenty rounds of this stupid card game like we saw today. Married! A decent worker has a higher salary than we do!"

His words completely saddened me. The beautiful day ended on a sour note; I drank more and more with him.

I mustn't socialize with him much. There is something ugly, Mephistophelean, in everything he says. The worst thing is that he does not speak cynically but quite calmly, as if all this goes without saying. Today I hate him.

From tomorrow a new schedule: I will stay at home, have dinner with my landlady, not go out, and study.

Enough procrastination!

Chapter V

The clock struck eight o'clock when Andrijašević hurried to enter his classroom from the small gymnasium hallway. The hallway has only one large window looking out on a small yard, so on days like today, when there was a bura with rain, it was dark and uncomfortable. The noise of children climbing the stairs, the smell of mud and the damp, and the walls simply smeared with white paint—create an atmosphere of tension and suffocation. Andrijašević never liked to stand in that corridor where the only decoration was an ancient clock built into the wall when Latin or German were still taught.

Besides, he did not want to run into his colleagues. He had already noticed some time before that associating with them led to quiet disagreements that occasionally grew stronger, giving birth to coldness. In particular, he could not stand the philologist, Maričić, a dry, ugly man of thirty, who, when the days were chillier, came to school wholly swathed in scarves. Đuro struggled to justify the unpleasant sides of Maričić's character, his malice, and insidiousness, which were the consequences of a

99

malady. At school, Maričić found constant irritations. He taught the seventh grade, which is why Andrijašević stuck with him keenly, even despite himself.

The reason was 'stupidity,' as Lukačevski described the whole thing. Two weeks before, Maričić, after reviewing homework, very rudely insulted Maras, a talented and lively student who understood everything except Greek philology. Maras began to reply; Maričić lost his composure and rudely spoke of the student's family of origin (Maras was the son of poor shepherds somewhere around Vratnik).

The matter came before the Board—and Maričić energetically demanded an exacting punishment since Maras unmistakably replied to the teacher, telling him he would not stand for Maričić insulting his parents. Đuro's other colleagues remained silent and went on correcting homework; Lukačevski chuckled contentedly, watching Maričić fly into a rage and call for the 'strictest procedures.' Andrijašević, who loved the open-minded and mature boy, opposed this and even accused Maričić of tactlessly provoking the conflict. A quarrel ensued, interrupted by the others; but after that, Maričić no longer wanted to talk with Andrijašević. That was not all: Đuro soon noticed that two other colleagues, Žuvić and Radović, agreed with Maričić and began looking at him with hostility.

This didn't bother him much (Lukačevski angered him by telling him after the conference: "You didn't remember any of my advice. What did you need that argument for? If the brat gets eight or sixteen hours—who cares; but you will still be saddled with trouble because of that stupidity!"); after the night he spent with Lukačevski, he barricaded himself in his room and started studying. Loneliness tormented him—and especially the days with bad weather took its toll. Yet he did not give up and, within a month, he had finished a good part of his study; he asked for a deadline for the exam, transcribed the dissertation and submitted it for approval. He forced himself into perseveration and resilience—and spent hours dreaming of Vera.

The day before, he had found out something that left him feeling very uncomfortable. In a newspaper, he noticed Vera's name among the ladies participating in a charity bazaar.

"They're sending her to parties! Before, she was neither allowed nor willing to do so without my permission; now, everything is different. And I can't even write to her about it!"

In the evening, he could not finish his usual task and squandered the whole time reading an English mystery novel that he happened to have. Barely had he been in class for a couple of hours (it was also dark there, especially the first hour in the morning, hardly at dusk) when a servant came and summoned him to the headmaster.

"Thank God—This will take a few moments—I am in no shape today to work in the classroom anyway."

*

The headmaster's room was the most beautiful and brightest in the building. As a person who was orderly and the son of an officer, the headmaster arranged his office as well as he could: there were red curtains on the

windows, somewhat tattered but nicely tucked into va-
lences; on the walls hung a pair of official paintings; two
bookcases and a wide desk filled only half the space.
Otherwise, everything shone with cleanliness, and even
the files on the table were arranged geometrically.

Upon entering, Andrijašević saw the headmaster light
a cigar with a solemn gesture. In general, he did everything pompously and properly; he was perpetually concerned about whether his conduct matched his standing
in this town where he was legitimately considered number two after the bishop. This is why he came into little
or no contact with the teachers outside of school; he
believed himself to be an aristocrat who should be only
hobnob with the county prefect and senior forester. He
dressed like a sportsman, so even now, he was all done
up in green loden; the same cloth was used for his cape
and hat. Đuro could not, until now, understand this
man; his colleagues also knew little about him because
he had been transferred to Senj only a few months earlier and always kept to himself. The only thing that cir-
culated about him was that the higher–ups appreciated
him and that a more important position awaited him in
the future.

"Ah, the servant misunderstood me—I did not wish
to disturb you while you were teaching, nor was it my
intention to have you come at once. So be it. Take a
seat. Were you teaching a sixth-grade class?"

"No, fourth."

"The fourth? So will the children be noisy? Hope-
fully, they will not. I, dear colleague (it was a habit of the
headmaster's to call subordinates "dear colleague"; he

thought this was very refined), I have been wanting to speak with you for several days. Please take it as if I were a friend, an older friend, and not your boss. It is not my custom to overdo things or give orders."

"Please go ahead."

(Andrijašević took and lit the cigarette offered; the headmaster always had a box of Egyptians handy, but he smoked cheap cigars).

"So listen to what I have to say. I attended one of your lectures and must compliment your deep interest in the subject you teach. I noticed your effort and seriousness; of course, I can say nothing about whether your progress will be commensurate to your efforts. Teaching is a tricky business that requires a lot of experience. For example, I noticed that sometimes you dig too deeply and with too much detail into a problem. Do you intend to prove that psychology is a bit too difficult for gymnasium? You are right, and this is why it is crucial to stick to the books and regulations dictated by the higher authorities so that we do not lose sight of the primary intention and purpose of our instruction. You are still—how shall I put this?—you may still be too full of memories of your own university lectures, and would like to explain any subject to my charges in depth and eloquently. Did you, yourself, notice how difficult this was?"

"It's true; some of them understand very little."

"Most, most of them, my dear colleague. In this way, it is difficult, if not impossible, to achieve the level of secondary education that the curriculum prescribes. So it is best to stick strictly to the book and call for at least a little more memorization ..."

"But psychology..."

"Listen, please, dear colleague. Do you think I don't believe that a complicated subject can be understood that way? But this can be achieved only with the most outstanding students, and we are dealing not only with average but also very weak students. The weakness of what we're dealing with forces us to make modifications (the headmaster importantly inhaled the smoke and set his cigar on an ash tray, while studying the ring on his finger). Besides—I must also tell you this—you have been carried away a couple of times by explaining to the students something that is not related to the subject, something that is not even mentioned in the recommended school book..."

Andrijašević felt the headmaster look at him and was embarrassed.

"Yes, they told me, and I saw it myself—you often veer off into other disciplines, you are too easily misled by the questions that students ask the teacher—and these questions serve one purpose only, to waste school time. If I am well informed, you spoke about the problem of matter, and you seem to have gone too far."

"I believed I was to teach science according to my current understanding."

"Again, you forget that we are dealing with middle-school students; in reality, most of them are below this level. They will either fail to grasp what you're saying or take what you say the wrong way, and your words will be interpreted as standing in conflict... in conflict with theories in other subjects. Do you understand me?"

"In short, I should stick to the book?"

"I did not want to spoil your enthusiasm; it is laudable that you are so interested in your subject and know more than is needed for the narrowest limits prescribed for training in psychology in a gymnasium. But, dear colleague, do not forget where we are. We are in a small town where everybody knows everything, and people talk about anything that comes to hand; where there is a lot of talk about something, there is a lot of misunderstanding. We are in a town with a bishop's seat."

Only now did everything become clear to Andrijašević. "Ah, so that's it! Someone feared that the children would begin questioning the stories about the soul, that is it!"

"This conversation, please, will remain between us. I appreciate you very much, dear colleague, I know your work outside of school, and I am always ready to support you. But please, do me a favor and do not get too carried away—this could only hurt you and there's no real benefit for the school. Our work, like the work of true teachers, should agree with all the factors on which successful school training depends, and above all this is religious education. That is what I wanted to tell you, dear colleague, and I ask you to act accordingly."

*

"Great way to start a day! As if I don't have enough trouble. I've been spending so much time alone, I'm not going out, I don't talk with anyone, I study and work. I have no friends, nor do I attend parties. The only thing that has cheered me a little was the school—and precisely those lectures on psychology, and they now want to take that away from me."

"So what did I do wrong? The students asked me about Haeckel—and I told them quite clearly that Haeckel was not a philosopher and that his book on the universe's riddles was full of inaccuracies and bold combinations. But yes—I added that it was appropriate for a scientist to criticize how this or that religion approaches the riddle of existence. Transcendental problems cannot be solved with the help of our ordinary principles. That, my God, is such an old and well-known thing!"

"Something is not right either. He says: I heard, I'm informed. Who did he hear from? So—they're stalking me. Still!"

"And if they only knew how far I am from a materialistic worldview!"

"What am I saying? Who cares what I think about the fundamental problems of philosophy? Maričić or someone else—this very headmaster with his *quasi-aristocratic* manners—and Radović with his misery—who among all these people knows anything about Kant or Mach! It is enough for them that I am, I don't even know why, unappealing—and they intend to harm me."

I also want to clarify that I was cautious when digging deeper into an issue—not to come into conflict "with religious education," as the headmaster so nicely put it. Lukačevski is right: we do not belong here. I am alien to them, and therefore I make them uncomfortable. The headmaster does not understand that you are going beyond the textbook, yet it seems essential to Maričić to preserve his authority as a corporal would."

"This is a big sacrifice for me. If I weren't obligated to Vera, I don't know if I would permit them ever again to talk down to me like that."

All that morning, Andrijašević did nothing but let the kids have fun any way they liked. He paced back and forth around the classroom, thinking and looking out the windows at the rain, hitting the glass hard.

After his classes were done, his colleague Rajčić met him in the hallway and invited him to come home with him for dinner.

"Gračar will also come so that it will be cheerful. And besides, colleague, you fraternize too seldom with us."

*

Andrijašević was glad to be invited. He knew that talking to the headmaster had ruined his whole day, so he would not be studying in the evening. Over the last few days, he had had to force himself to stay in his room and not go out after dinner. He began to bribe himself as a child would—he asked for tea to be brewed for him before he went to bed.

The longing for Vera was more painful than ever. He felt the weight of his commitment more and more, promising not to approach her until he had finished his exams. He realized that passing the exam would take far longer than he'd initially thought; he estimated he would go to Zagreb in the fall. Having become better acquainted with his current job, he knew that even after a year, he would not be appointed to even the lowest full position.

And the days went by far too slowly. He could not associate with Lukačevski because he was frightened by the awful emphasis with which this man spoke about the downfall of those who dedicated themselves to the professorial class in the province. He knew the other colleagues only from official interactions; a few of them truly disgusted him. About the others, whom he had initially regarded as attractive, he started to believe that they, too, were subject to the faults that life brings to those in the narrow confines of a small town.

Rajčić was one of these. He used to be one of the best students at the university, so even then, he still participated in philological discussions in specialized journals. He was conscientious and punctual in his teaching, which is why they forgave his well-known drinking problem. The same Maričić, a few days after they met, revealed Rajčić's weakness to Đuro and viciously added that this "does not agree at all with the duties of a teacher." Later, Đuro found out that Rajčić did not get along with his wife, who blamed him for marrying her. (She was the daughter of a wealthy merchant from the Northern regions; life with Rajčić could not match the prosperity in her childhood home.)

Before getting ready for the dinner, Đuro remembered that he did not know Rajčić's wife. "They have never asked me to stop by, and now all of a sudden I'm invited as a guest." It was not for the sake of the Rajčićes—he knew that it was not unusual for a first visit to be followed by an official one. Still, he rebuked himself for not remembering to wear a black suit earlier in the afternoon before going there.

"You see, I've already forgotten my social manners. Well, I can't help but go like this. And a black suit would be perhaps too formal."

To somehow mark his first visit, he went to pick up Gračar, thinking of entering Rajčić's house for the first time with him.

*

Gračar was one of the oldest married teachers and the father of five children. He lived farther off, on one of the smaller alleyways where the town started climbing the hill.

Andrijašević, under the blows of the rain that hadn't stopped and was icy in the evening, barely found the house. Climbing the stone steps of the yard, he came to a massive wooden door and knocked.

Gračar's wife opened the door herself—carrying her youngest son, a three-year-old, in her arms.

"Sorry to bother you so late; is your husband at home?"

Mrs. Gračar was dressed in barely more than a negligee; an old, worn-out skirt and a half-buttoned blouse made it clear that she was not expecting visitors. Đuro's visit did not seem to worry her at all; his colleague's wife appeared quite accustomed to such trappings and was not bothered that a stranger had found her in such disarray.

"Please come in—yes, he's home; he told me he had been invited to dinner by Rajčić; are you going too?"

In an instant, three more children appeared around Andrijašević; a five-year-old girl, all in tears, with a piece of bread in her mouth, and two half-naked boys.

"Come on, kids, off to bed. They got out of bed again. You know, Sir, there is never peace with children around."

Very kindly, and after asking about his health, Mrs. Gračar directed Đuro through the kitchen to "her husband's room." The kitchen was low, dimly lit by a small lamp hanging from the wall. Everything smelled of soap and laundry.

Hearing the kitchen door open, Gračar shouted from his room, "You're opening the door again! What's the matter with you today; I can feel the draft every time!"

But when Đuro showed up, he happily rose to his feet and offered his guest a seat. He was sitting in a well-heated room, correcting homework.

The room was called "his," as Mrs. Gračar had said; but it consisted of a dining room with a private corner for Gračar, furnished with only a bookcase and a tall, simple desk, resembling the place in the foyer of the office where the clerks sit. The leftovers from the children's dinner, crumbled bread and water spilled all over the leather table cover.

"It's a little messy here—but you have to forgive that. We are slaves to our children. And it's not easy to get them to behave when there are five of them. I was just getting dressed and ready to go."

Gračar immediately started dressing and joking about every piece of his suit. He had problems finding his cuffs. Although the search lasted quite a long time, he did not get angry but laughed at the children who were timidly watching the guest and did not leave the room.

Once out on the street, Gračar stopped Đuro in front of a street lamp.

"I have to warn you—don't be surprised if Mrs. Rajčić resents having us in or quarrels with her husband. That's how she is."

＊

That fear was not justified. Mrs. Rajčić greeted the guests very politely as if this were an official visit. She was a fairly young woman with well-defined features and a surprisingly low, soft voice. She dressed in a household outfit that must have long been stored in a closet waiting for formal occasions; inadvertently, Andrijašević thought of mothballs.

Rajčić was happy; it was undeniable that he had already had a little to drink before dinner, but the entrance went very nicely and cheerfully. After the visit to the Gračar family, Đuro especially liked the fact that the dining room of the Rajčić's was tastefully decorated—with the only furniture that remained after Rajčić's father's bankruptcy. The dinner was far more modest than the tableware, but Andrijašević conversed brightly.

Immediately after dinner, Rajčić began suggesting they raise their glasses and make toasts. His wife gave him an unkindly look two or three times, and in her quiet and soft voice she said that toasting was a horrible custom.

"You are never satisfied until you drink too much."

Rajčić immediately got up and began to celebrate, in an ornate speech, his dear guest, who was visiting his house for the first time. After half an hour, Đuro had already drunk a few full glasses and began treating both colleagues as if they were old friends.

Gračar was in extraordinarily high spirits.

"You are the most blessed man in the world—you are always ready to tell a joke," flattered Mrs. Rajčić, who kept getting ready to go off and make tea, but her husband warned her every time she got up that it was still too early for that.

"Dear madam, this is how it is: we state employees have no choice. Everything goes against us; no pay to speak of but needs aplenty; at school, always trouble, at home, always misery. Who could handle it all while also being in a foul mood? This is how we manage. Long live gallows humor!"

They all clinked glasses.

Gračar clucked his tongue and chuckled again.

"For us teachers, there are only two ways out of our situation. One is gallows humor, and the other would be this: for there to be a vote in parliament on a law by which a debtor is imprisoned for debts. I would do my two years—and then start living again. Eh, you'd see how happy I would be!"

Everyone laughed; only Mrs. Rajčić was not at all fond of this topic; she was deeply troubled by debts, her husband's wages had been expropriated a long time ago, and now she lived from one day to the next, hoping for salvation from a better position or income for revising outdated textbooks.

The conversation slowly turned to more serious matters. Rajčić began by complaining about his miserable circumstances and the exorbitant cost of living (his wife used this moment and started preparing the saucers and cups for tea) and finally told Đuro that he would like to ask him a question.

"Just don't ask for signatures; no one here will give you or me anything more on a promissory note," Gračar laughed out loud.

It was not about a promissory note. Rajčić spoke at length to Đuro about how he, Andrijašević, is a well-known literary name, how his books are valued—and finally asked him to write a review in a well-known literary magazine concerning a revised older textbook that Rajčić had just published.

Đuro already felt he had drunk a lot; not wanting to cause discontent, he promised everything Rajčić wanted and completely ignored the fact that he knew nothing of Rajčić's work, it had nothing to do with his qualifications and his praiseworthy review would be a little suspect.

Great joy now flourished. Rajčić immediately told his wife, who returned from the kitchen with tea, that "our great writer" was very pleased with his textbook and would announce his satisfaction to the "doltish public." He then immediately asked her to put away the tea and bring out a new bottle of wine.

His wife thanked Andrijašević, but she also started to let them know this was wrong and they had had too much to drink.

While Rajčić and Gračar tried in vain to perform a song as a duet (Gračar had taken off his glasses because, he said, he could now see things so clearly!), around midnight, she began holding forth to Andrijašević—who had been holding off on the wine for a while—how grueling the teaching profession is, how one must get up early, be fresh, not waste one's nights, and so forth.

Đuro understood and got up a quarter of an hour later to say goodbye.

But the others were by no means ready to depart so abruptly. Rajčić failed to persuade Đuro to stay, so he did not hesitate to tell his wife that her yawning was to blame for their guest's desire to leave.

Finally, Gračar, too, got up; but Rajčić immediately said they must go out for black coffee because the "*Madame* wants to sleep."

There then ensued an awkward scene: Mrs. Rajčić, in her soft and gentle voice, quite at odds with the harshness of her words, began chiding her husband: where was he going when he was so drunk? And she berated Gračar who, as an older man, should have known better. "That's all I need—to be a know-it-all after such a fine dinner!"

But Gračar's laughter did not silence the dissonance; a real fight developed over the house keys, and even worse, Rajčić had to beg his wife to give him money.

"I have no money—you drink everything anyway, and nothing is left from your salary."

Đuro grew more and more uncomfortable. Rajčić wouldn't let him go but instead, without a second thought, began arguing with his wife. Finally, he begged her to give him at least one crown; when she did not give him that either, he tried to snatch the keys from the armoire. Gračar continued eating and drinking philosophically while Đuro stood with hat in hand and had to watch Rajčić get closer to the woman and insult her more and more. She finally threw the keys onto the table, burst into sobs, and called him all sorts of derogatory names.

"Ah, why did I sacrifice my youth for such a nobody—you are not ashamed to be drunk even in front of guests" ... a whole sea of curses were heard through her sobs ...

Arriving home, Đuro did not want to lie down for a time. He paced around the room, smoking cigarette after cigarette, thinking this might calm him.

"How these people live, how these people live! Gračar is in fine spirits—and his wife is like a maid servant. How can he survive in that small room?"

"You're drunk, you good-for-nothing...," Mrs. Rajčić's quiet voice and her sobs kept ringing in his ears.

"The unfortunate man feted me and plied me with wine; he wants to be praised in the press. Yet the poor wretch cannot see how much he had to pay for my praise by arguing with her like that in front of me!"

"Now I don't even know if I dare visit them. How can I face Mrs. Rajčić again? Ah, alas—they probably feel no shame. Arguing in front of a stranger like that! It seemed nothing unusual for them; Gračar wasn't the slightest bit alarmed."

"Terrible, horrible. And in the end, he had to beg her for a crown! One crown! Maybe she really didn't have one. One of them is happy thinking about clearing his debts by going to prison; the other isn't ashamed to beg a woman in front of me for a few coins!"

"Poverty, misery. No surprise that they drink. I, too, was drunk. And I also promised to write a review."

"What keeps these people going, my God! Is such a life worth paying for with such torment?"

"Vera and Gračar's wife ... and Mrs. Rajčić. Colleagues ... colleagues' wives; is such a thing possible? ..."

Đuro remembered Vera's refined, stern appearance; he recalled life at her house, measured, comfortable, courteous ... and couldn't close his eyes the whole night.

Chapter VI

Slowly and regularly, the days flowed by. After a
beautiful spring, the gardens turned a rich green,
and small bushes and grass grew here and there on
the barren rocky countryside around Senj. The sun was
already beating down though it was only May.

Đuro was finding it harder to spend evenings in his
room with his books. The Dalmatian nights lured him
outdoors—and he could spend entire evenings walking
by the sea. His old habit of reliving the most impossible
combinations of events in his imagination possessed
him like never before. His love for Vera became more a
difficult and painful memory. Every day brought him
new disappointments: he was increasingly bored at
school since he had been forced to stop his free conversation with the students and stick to a dry pattern of as-
signing and reviewing lessons. Material worries plagued
him every day; worst of all, he had to constantly convince himself that there would never be an end to the
scarcity of money that tormented all his colleagues as
much as it worried him. He did not dare to think about
or seriously consider marrying Vera; he gave in to

thoughts that something ought to change or that something unexpected would come along to fix all his troubles.

The decision to 'surrender to life' was nothing new for him. Whenever an issue arose that could not be immediately overcome or was inconsistent with his mentality of longing for harmony and peace, or every time he found himself face to face with the problems of ordinary life that could not be dispelled by thoughts or dreams, Andrijašević passively concluded that there was no point in banging one's head, and—he waited to see what would transpire. There was a hidden belief in the depths of his soul that happiness, for him, was not in the stars—and this belief turned into fatalism as soon as Andrijašević found an obstacle in his path for which he was not responsible. Unable to admit this, he became increasingly reconciled to the idea that he should succumb to all the troubles that had befallen him—there was no point in fighting because there was no hope of success. He was still doing his part and practiced for his exam every day. Yet, at the slightest mental displeasure, he would reluctantly throw down the book and flee from his room, saying to himself: One day more or one day less, it does not matter; I can do it for as long as I think Vera will be mine.

And the very thought of "when Vera will be mine" slowly, one step a day, floated further away. He looked at his married colleagues, at their misery, their habits; he realized he could not stay solvent now or in the future with his salary or the salary he would receive later. Vera was becoming an uncatchable creature; a comfortable life in her family, the habits of people who have enough to afford some luxury—all of these were so unlike his current situation, as, in vain, he sought a way out.

As a student in Vienna, he had lived quite well; his uncle's support, scholarships, and a little something for small needs and his literary work provided a monthly income that was enough for a reasonably good life. Since childhood, he had been not used to great abundance, so in ordinary things, especially eating, he easily limited himself to the strict necessities. He didn't mind having only a piece of ham and bread with tea for dinner. But he was far more accustomed to another luxury: attending theater plays and exhibitions and following the latest music news. The interaction with Vera's family brought him another problem: his wardrobe.

And—strange! In the big city, he made ends meet and Đuro was happy with his life. However, here there were almost none of the parties and entertainments he had spent a good part of his money on in Vienna; yet his deprivation grew daily. Đuro had already written three times to his mother asking for money; the second time, she seemed to be sending it against her better judgment, and the third time he had to go to see her in Rijeka. The business about Toma's legacy went very poorly; it turned out that the house needed repairs, and a good portion of the cash left by Toma was being used for that. His mother could not quite understand why Đuro needed "so much money" since he was now done with schooling and on his own; she was attending more and more church services and distancing herself from the world, becoming less attuned to the needs of everyday life. She could hardly afford to give him even a small sum.

With all that, by the beginning of June, Đuro was in serious trouble. He was surprised by how much money it took to lead such a miserable life. But a simple list of expenses showed him that, what with housing, food, charitable contributions, paying off a small student loan, and petty necessities, he was seventy crowns above his 'salary.' He did not add to this the clothing purchased with the money 'borrowed' from his mother. The expense report was clear; the deficit was more significant than all the money he could possibly obtain. He thought for a moment about looking for tutoring opportunities, but at the end of the school year there were none—and other than tutoring, there were no other ways to earn money. On June 1, it occurred to him that he had to pay his landlady half of the money for food and lodging—and yet he had nothing left in his pocket.

This bothered him more than anything else. He, a grown man, was ashamed to tell the poor grandmother, the secretary's widow, 'I'll pay you later.' Grandma said not a word, but two days later, when she came to his room, Đuro found this difficult and awkward.

"Ah, if I were in a big city, it would be easy. You reduce costs for one-two months, move to a cheaper place, save on food—and everything goes well again. In two or three months, you move from one district to another, avoid your friends—and everything is taken care of. Where could I escape from here? Professor—you must have dinner; you can't save on the apartment, you can't pawn your suit—and what is left are costs that can't be reduced."

Halfway through the month, he was troubled by a shortage of cash. On the fifteenth, the landlady told him she was poor and had to stop feeding him unless he paid her; she forced Andrijašević to give her his last ten forints—and he still owed more. He was left with three crowns in his pocket and was quite alarmed; he was afraid to go into society to reveal his sad circumstances.

He began taking long walks, more out of necessity than genuine desire. Twice he invited Gračar to join him for a walk to a nearby village; but after that, he had to go alone because the walk ended both times with a visit to a country inn where he had to spend his last pittance.

Yet the out-of-doors was beautiful. Long stone roads, rugged and winding, went along the sea in two directions. From the northwest and to the southwest spread the views of the sea, changing by the minute.

As a cloud moves, as the sun rises or the light dies, the sea changes hue. In the morning, it is almost the same as the sky, so you can't see the boundaries between the endless water, the rugged island, and the horizon. It is smooth—and the bare pink gorges are reflected in it as in a mirror. Along the coast, the sea is light green; further away, gray. The near-by shadows are a translucent, dark green, the distant ones purple and intense. But only in the evening do the seas reveal all their beauty. A bloody sun sets behind the island, which loses its three-dimensional shape and juts on the horizon like a dark, sharply contoured bulk. Each wave floats like a ruddy pearl—each sail reflected in a hundred shivering shades of rouge. And on the other side: a stone ridge, gloomy and monotonous as if clenching its teeth in preparation for death. There are no houses on it or people—it climbs high in a hunched line—all the way to the top of Velebit, covered with a light fog.

Late in the evening, Đuro returned from his walks at a steady pace, not taking in the individual aspects of nature's beauty, but enjoying the whole magnificent picture, composed of the soft and warm colors of the sea and the desolate solitude of the uninhabited crags. All this transported him into a kind of ecstasy in which he would completely lose his sense of the moment—and reflected, fantasized without boundaries.

From his earliest youth, he had been a dreamer. The actual patterns of life never interested him much—so he was left with the actions of others and public action and all those things, which people stuffed under the broad heading of the social sciences. His imagination could not bear the shackles of beauty for itself alone; although he was thrilled by the harmony of color and line, images, thoughts, and rationales arranged themselves in his soul abruptly, touching all possible things. He remembered that, as a boy, he dreamed for days about what suddenly becoming rich would be like. And now similar thoughts came to mind—and serious reflection crept into his reveries. This would send him musing on the probability of winning the lottery and how he'd arrange his life if he had an income of five or ten thousand forints a year. In his imagination, he would choose different forms of prosperity: traveling, living quietly by a beautiful lake in a splendid villa, fantasizing about his literary vocation, his unpublished books, the pleasures of music, and the comforts of life for people who do not have to worry about their daily bread. Another time he would be entirely bewildered by the news of a technological advancement—and he would immediately think of himself as a great craftsman of artificial gemstones or of a perfect machine. Merchants flock to him; his product is treasured, he sells it—he'd be the director of a vast company with a thousand workers, a famous man. Or: he writes a play, a work that amazes people. He can almost see the actors in a colossal scene in which a new Nero, the ruler of the Paris Stock Exchange, sacrifices a thousand lives. He can hear the silence and the tension of the audience holding their breath—and then the applause, the thrill, the intoxication. He is famous, rich, respected... a world-famous publisher offers him a large annuity in return for publishing his works...

In these endless fantasies, Andrijašević stepped away from the reality of his current, unpleasant life. It never occurred to him to start something (he did regularly buy lottery tickets), to produce something in the literary field—his world of imagination existed in and of itself, and Đuro always sought it when he needed to escape reality's troubles.

*

And these accumulated day by day. At home, he was increasingly bored; he did not dare to ask the landlady to buy him the small things he had been reimbursing her for until this month. He was late with his student loan repayment and immediately received a letter from a lawyer. He felt the need for conversation, to join his colleagues for a while, to cheer himself up (he had already been declared an oddball, an outcast, a snob)—and could not bring himself to go to the inn where he owed a couple of glasses of beer. When Rajčić once ran into him on the street and invited him over "for a glass of conversation," he did not hesitate, even though he was not keen to visit Rajčić's wife after that dinner. This time Mrs. Rajčić greeted him coldly, but Đuro was nevertheless happy to spend the evening in company. After all, Mrs. Rajčić's sour mood was not so evident once two ladies, her sister and a town teacher, joined the company.

Andrijašević liked the latter. She was long past the age of thirty, but it never occurred to anyone to mock her for being a spinster: she did not hide her age, was in fine spirits, and was happy to have a good time. Her attitude and age gave her a freedom that is not typically allowed for younger women in a small town; besides, everyone respected her, and—as with any grammar school teacher—almost everyone was friendly with her. Miss Darinka lived a pleasant and happy life and kept most of her spare time for socializing and amateur theatricals; she preferred to play old ladies; she was a member of the reading room where she often came to read the newspaper.

Always ready to take advantage of a new acquaintance, Darinka immediately suggested to Andrijašević that they should create a standing amateur society, with him running the administration. Đuro barely escaped her ploy, to which she, supposedly offended and with comic resignation, rebuked the big city denizens who did not care to fraternize 'with us snails.'

"You are a young gentleman—and we have so many lively young girls, so it is not right that you live alone as you do. Join us for a while, and you will see that we are not so primitive."

In the end, he had to promise her that he would take part in a trip to a nearby village, where Darinka with two other young girls, and Mr. Rajčić, Mrs. Rajčić, and two other gentlemen, would visit one of Darinka's friends from school.

The trip date was chosen for the first of two holidays at the end of the month. Two days before, Andrijašević realized he would need money for the excursion.

"But I guess I'll dig up five forints somewhere," he comforted himself and went first to Gračar. "He won't have the money, but at least he'll know how to advise me."

But Gračar turned out to be very worried.

"Five forints! Listen, friend, that's a lot. I don't have a penny myself, I barely have any cigars left. Wait, maybe we'll find some colleagues ..."

Đuro did not want to ask anyone other than Rajčić.

"Oh, he doesn't have the money for sure, and if by chance there is any money in his house, you know, his wife, not he, is the one who would have it. Why do you need money?"

Đuro explained.

"Hmmm—for a trip, I guess that's not such a critical need."

"For God's sake, five forints is not much of a sum!"

"After the twentieth in the month, it's more than thirty is on the first. If only you could wait until the end of the semester, people get exam fees. And what about Lukačevski?"

"I haven't spoken with him for ages. I'd rather not ask him."

"It's your fault that everything is so difficult for you now; you don't socialize with anyone. You know what— try asking the headmaster."

"Ah, please, if he refuses me, I would have to curse him." They finally agreed that they would try with other colleagues. Gračar took this upon himself and went first to the two he thought should have money. In the evening, he told Đuro he had failed.

"There is no other choice but to ask Žuvić. He'll lend it to you. He likes when people are obliged to him. He is counting on becoming the next headmaster." Andrijašević had a difficult time deciding. He mustered the courage, however, and that morning, between classes, he asked Žuvić for the favor.

"Well, well, you need money. And we thought you were doing so well. You don't socialize with anyone; you live all by yourself, so we didn't expect you to come when you needed something from any of us. Regrettably, I can't help you, but know what—try Maričić ... And, you somehow don't look your best; shall I ask on your behalf?"

"No, I don't want a humiliation," thought Đuro, thanked Žuvić and sent Miss Darinka a post that he was ill and could not accompany her on the trip.

Because of this, he was stuck at home for two vacation days. The room was humid and uncomfortable.

What's worse, the landlady took his illness seriously and completely forgot that Andrijašević owed her part of the rent and that she had already reminded him twice. So she started caring for him: she wanted to force him to drink milk and see a doctor. The next day he couldn't stand it any longer and went straight to the inn in the evening.

"Why! In Vienna, I was in debt to other people so many times; I will be able to do the same here."

*

"Look—the convalescent!" Lukačevski greeted him, half worried, half-mocking. "How is it? I heard you were sick—so you didn't go on the trip with the Rajčićes."

"Ah, nothing, a minor indisposition!"

"Just be careful not to make her mad at you. Miss Darinka does not like men who do not obey her." (Ðuro caught a malevolent edge in these words.)

"I hardly know her and the others, so they must have had a good time even without me."

"Who knows? After all, you were the only man she invited, and there were three young ladies! ..."

"Come on, please."

Lukačevski was in surprisingly high spirits. Ðuro, a little embarrassed, ordered the first glass, thinking that in the end, he would have to tell the waitress to wait until the first of the month; but little by little he forgot, and he didn't go home for dinner 'so he wouldn't owe just a few coins.'

"But that is as it should be, stay with me for a while. Gračar will come later; today is a holiday, so he couldn't live without his post-prandial half-liter. *À propos*—I wanted to tell you something—do not misunderstand me. You did yourself a disservice by asking for money the other day."

"How do you know that?"

"How do I know? My friend, everyone knows. What is not known here? And the people you turned to aren't exactly the kind who will protect you and be discreet. Žuvić beamed with pleasure, telling me that you admitted it is poor form to ignore colleagues and then come begging. Did he at least give you what you were asking for?"

"No."

"I knew it. He had it but wanted to humiliate you all the more—by sending you to ask Maričić. That was careless on your part. He will carve you to pieces, make a hundred from a penny, and do you harm. Why didn't you come to me? Are you getting married? I ask because you haven't been with me for such a long time. I know that. You didn't like me judging so candidly about all this misery we all find ourselves in. Be patient—you will soon be lamenting, and this will bring comfort. I always have a pair of crowns; not more. I am poor and must maintain strict discipline so that what happened to you does not happen to me. I would not go begging Žuvić, nor would I want to be obligated to him. It's the worst of all things—to be obliged to someone at our school. Do you know where you can borrow without fear? Here. See, this waitress is the most honest of creatures. She's here day in and day out, so she doesn't worry much about it. Another waitress will come—and the first lets the second know of the amount. She won't tell anyone—and no need to be embarrassed at owing ten crowns. Take this as a rule: you can have as many debts as you like, but not where you work. I have suits made in Pest—and I pay in endless installments. And the fellow in the big city will wait—what are your five forints to him? He doesn't care whether he gets them this month or the next! But if Rajčić, who is, after all, an honest man, lends you a forint—you must return it to him within eight days because otherwise he cannot pay for his cigarettes."

"A forint, five forints! Marvelous. We have come to the same position I heard about that night at the Rajčić's: haggling over a crown." That evening, Andrijašević was not upset by Lukačevski's harsh criticism or his cynicism.

"He's right: it's all such a terrible misfortune; this cannot get much worse."

*

The very next day, Andrijašević took up a pencil to write out his budget. On one side he wrote all his sources of income—his meager salary and the small amount he could still expect from his mother; while on the other, his expenses and debts. The result of the calculation was that it was impossible to survive on his income. "This month, I'm already in deficit with housing and food; next month, the deficit will increase; what will happen then? I'll have to borrow money as an IOU—and I won't be able to repay; in one—or two years I will accumulate so much debt that my situation will not improve even if I keep my teaching appointment."

He didn't dare to think about marriage, about Vera—for now, the main thing was to get out of these dire straits; on the first of the month one has to pay all arrears—and a hundred crowns cannot be divided among many creditors. So he decided to write to his mother and ask for money, even though the last time she gave him some it was begrudgingly; besides, as soon as he paid off some of his debts, he would arrange for her to come to him in Senj.

"It would be easier if we lived together and more comfortable for me. After all, it is not nice for my mother to host students in her apartment so she can afford to buy food. I will write her to come to Senj immediately after the first of the month."

He liked that thought. He did not stop to think that they might relocate him to another school after the holidays or that his mother might not be so eager to replace her ordinary life with a new, unknown one. As if his whole future truly depended on this decision, Đuro wrote a long enthusiastic letter to his mother, explaining his financial difficulties, acknowledging her skills in frugality and running a household, sparked a few memories from his childhood, and achingly pleaded with her to come "to her son who feels so lonely." After reading the letter, he was pretty satisfied and calculated that his mother would have it in her hands the next day and would surely respond immediately.

Indeed, the mother's letter did arrive forthwith. In three or four dry sentences, as if she were reluctant to provide more detail, she informed her son that she could neither come now nor later nor could she send money.

"My dear son, I thought you had finished your studies and should no longer rely on outside help. I would never come to you to ask you for anything but your filial loyalty. This is why I decided as follows for the little remaining time I have to live: I donated Toma's house, together with the cash he left behind, to our abbey monastery; because of this legacy, the nuns will feed me until I die, and after death, an eternal Mass will be read for the salvation of my soul. Your needs for money, dear Đuro, certainly could not be so urgent; and when I did as I have described, this soothed my conscience and took care of the salvation of my soul to enjoy greater than carnal goods. Therefore I inform you that I cannot come to you. I'm already old and do want to pretend to be a lady, which I'd have to do if I moved as your mother to a small town."

At first, Đuro was furious. He wondered why his mother had decided to give Toma's house as a gift (of course, with all the debts) without consulting her son.

"She is getting old, no doubt; she has become a habitué of the church, her mind is failing, they have brainwashed her!—If only she had not given them the cash! And now she has reduced me to such straits!"

But he was a little ashamed of his reproaches. His mother had had no other thoughts all her life than to strive for him, to make his life as easy as possible. And now he resented her for deciding to devote the end of her life to prayer, leaving a few hundred for a Mass!

"It's my fault it happened this way. I haven't written to her for a whole year. I only sent her a postcard when I needed money. Of course, that hurt her and she found solace all the more in the church."

"It's only that I now have a major problem in getting rid of these little debts. And where am I going on vacation? If the house is already donated, I can't ask for hospitality from my mother. Everything is so final."

Lukačevski himself, to whom Đuro confided his financial woes, could not solve this problem either.

"If you have nowhere to go on vacation, it's easy; you stay here, repay something, and then take up another loan. If you have to leave, then it is challenging because you need cash. But we'll see on the first of the month."

*

On the first of the month in the afternoon, just as Đuro was handing the landlady his penultimate forint for the debt, the gymnasium janitor brought him a telegram.

"Who's wiring me? ... Did my mother have an accident?" He was almost afraid to open it. Inside he read the words:

"Come to Zagreb now. I need to talk to you.— Vera."

"Please sign," the janitor pushed him the receipt across the table. At first, Andrijašević did not understand; a telegram, after long, long months, the word from Vera moved him so that he could not tear his eyes from the blue letters. He was overcome by emotion, almost in tears.

Left alone, he sat down at the table and let his feelings overtake his mind—just as he learned to close his eyes and immerse himself in music, without organized thoughts, as if borne by a wave moving him forward.

... "Vera! Vera! My precious girl! It must be difficult for you; you want me to be with you ...."

He saw her: serious, beautiful, with all the modesty of her gestures, with eyes that looked at him so brightly and confidently. It seemed to him that those eyes were now weeping, careworn, looking for help and hope in him.

Nothing, nothing could turn you away from me—you are my girl—beautiful, good, lovely ... and in his mind, he expressed his love for her with the most beautiful words, he almost felt that she was nearby, he stroked her hair, leaned his head on her shoulder.

It was as if Vera's worries, which he sensed from the telegram, had pierced him. He wanted to hold her, take her hand, whisper to her that he was with her—and that he wouldn't let her go ...

But mixed with that feeling was the realization of his own misery and helplessness. Weakness, almost despair, gripped his soul.

"Ah, how miserable we are—and you, my poor thing."

Compassion for Vera's suffering no longer came from a man who was pleased that she was asking him for help—in his feelings, Andrijašević moved closer to her pain and drowned in it with Vera. Scenes of their love intertwined with the impressions of his current lonely, dreary, meaningless life until it became more and more evident that his current situation was hopeless...

With the sighs of a half-resigned man, he rose from the table when dusk was already well advanced...

"It's all so awful and ludicrous. That she has to send me telegrams like this, most likely in secrecy—and the next day she will be waiting for me somewhere at a corner, ashamed—in hiding…"

He was ashamed for her, thinking she would be waiting for him impatiently on the street, looking around to ensure that no one noticed her, as if there were something wrong with her …

"And I'm going to have to tell her that life is terrible for me too. Where can I find the words to comfort her—and ask for her patience … Another year … and longer… It will be all over once I take that exam."

He didn't want to let his thoughts drift any further. He saw himself and her, embraced during their infrequent private encounters; he remembered Gračar and Mrs. Rajčić, all those miserable and failed people who became ugly and repulsive because misery made them so …

"What a reunion this will be! Now, just months after I left Vienna …"

"And why is she wiring me? A suitor must have asked for her hand, one who would press her to forget me. They offer her wealth, luxury, and a life without worries."

"Poor thing—what can I offer?"

His thoughts were so heavy that Đuro could not bear to spend the evening between four walls. As things lost color and shape and sank into an indefinite black-gray combination, his gloom and fear took hold.

Late dusk had settled in. On the road to Velebit, the last strollers returned to town ahead of the darkness approaching from afar in vast areas. The sky and the sea acquired the same serene hue, and the bare crags, as far as the eye could see, looked like a colossal monument to all the buried hopes, all the lost joy.

"Yes, I must go to her tomorrow ... It's good that I at least have a decent suit ... Pretty soon, I will not have the means to worry about that. Tomorrow ... But how?"

It was painful to think of the need to find the money for the trip because something deep in his heart told him this would not be possible.

"Lukačevski will have it... Gračar also raised his fee because of his non-obligatory Italian training. The trip is cheap ... it will be enough to stay in Zagreb for two days. Thirty forints will do it ... ah, twenty-five ... That much will easily be found ..."

*

Đuro did not leave the next day or the day after. He was upset for two days, thinking: I will not survive this, I will go mad.

The first evening he came to the inn and asked Lukačevski for money. Lukačevski immediately challenged him with his calm gaze, thought for a moment, and said:

"No, friend. This month I had bills to pay. You can't go on vacation if you don't pay. They would think I ran away. Who knows if I'll still be working here a year from now? And I'd rather sacrifice I don't know what, than be hunted down or gossiped about. Only in this way can you maintain independence. I don't have much. I can give you five forints."

But even those five forints did not remain long in Andrijašević's hands. As they were leaving the inn, Lukačevski noticed the waitress looking at them askance and he warned Đuro. She remembered he had not paid since the previous month. It was necessary to settle his tab.

His friend comforted him, saying he might find the money tomorrow. But Gračar stated that his earnings from Italian were pledged three months ago to the bank for a debt. Lukačevski had not lost hope yet, and he helped Đuro. But all efforts were in vain.

"Now is the worst time, everyone is getting ready for the holidays, and they are paying their debts as much as they can."

They tried with the headmaster; he held himself very officially and stated that "there is no title" for an advance. Andrijašević couldn't bear to continue listening and almost ran from the room. Other efforts also failed. Đuro humbled himself and went to implore Maričić, but Maričić insulted him by telling him that he would never have come to Andrijašević with such a request "after what happened."

"You're a bastard!" Đuro told him in anger and left. Lukačevski tried to persuade a merchant to sign an IOU, but this would take a couple of days, and he was unlikely to sign it anyway.

On the third day, Đuro, after a futile outing, humiliation, and torment, slumped into total apathy. He would take out the telegram, look at it for the hundredth time—and put it back into his pocket.

He tried to console himself with all sorts of imaginary excuses.

"Maybe it's nothing serious; Vera probably went to the telegraph office in a rush of love—otherwise, she would have written, she wouldn't have wired. I'll write something and go after I get paid in two months; yes, I'll definitely go to Zagreb."

Still, he couldn't regain his composure. On the fourth day, he was left alone (Lukačevski, too, was gone) and with nothing to do. He was assailed by a lethargy he could not shake no matter what he tried. At night, unable to sleep (he had already spent the third night half awake), he rose and wrote Vera a letter. He didn't even dwell on his writing; he held the pages almost feverishly for a long time. He described his life to her (but was careful not to point out his misery), talked about the exam because of which he must stay in Senj over the holidays to study—he wrote words of love that he rarely let leave his pen and finally begged her to be patient.

He mailed it immediately. On the third day, he received it, returned unopened. He immediately guessed that old Hrabarova had received it. Indeed she recognized his handwriting and sent the letter back in a new envelope, unopened.

*

In Senj, July 7

My dear Toša!

I must ask you for a great favor; this is so important that you must not turn me down.

(He briefly described his relationship with Vera and added a request for Toša to go to Zagreb, to try in any possible way to get in touch with Vera, to deliver to her the attached letter, and to inquire about what happened to the Hrabars, to enquire about why she had sent the telegram).

So please—don't say no. You can easily find the money to go to Zagreb and do this for me. I cannot.

I don't want to write more about myself. I cannot. Everything is so difficult and unpleasant; when I think about myself, all goes dark before my eyes. I'll just tell you this: my Toša, I do not belong here with these people. Why, I do not know; but I know that for my life, I need a particular situation, not a rich and luxurious one, but a milieu where I don't stumble at every step. The people now around me have only one goal in life: to ensure their daily bread. And, that doesn't seem to work for them, either. Nor for me. Is it my fault that so far I have moved beyond the boundaries provided by our society, or is this someone else's fault—about this I can't make a sound judgment. The only thing I know is that I feel terrible. In my job and for the people, I find no support to learn how to face the ordinary, tedious issues that are the first necessities of life. Given my ridiculous salary, on the other hand, I cannot obtain anything for myself, for my spiritual life. And as to the future—what foundations can be built?

I am condemned to stay here over the holidays. Will I ever get out of here, will that change?

Ah, you are happy! I envy you. And you pity me— and don't let me down with what I am asking you to do. This is the only thing that keeps me together. Please greet everyone nicely and cordially—and I greet you,

Đuro

P.S. Go now and answer immediately. I am sick from the anxiety and the expectation.

*

Fugue

Zagreb, 21 August

Dear Đuka!

Your letter did not find me in Zdenci where you sent it. We have a new son, and my old man—for the sake of his grandson—reconciled with Anka, so we are with them for the holidays. That's why I got your letter only this month (God knows how long the village headman kept it with him)! I could only now go to Zagreb because I want a transfer closer to my father; otherwise, I will give up my job.

I did as you wished and asked around. Well, in fact I did not ask anything but went straight to Hrabar's apartment, thinking this would be the best course of action. I made up a story about a teachers' union (Miss Vera is, as I found out, a licensed teacher), so I was hoping to speak with her and give her your letter. However, I did not find the Hrabars. The caretaker told me that Miss Vera fell ill in July and the whole family went for treatment somewhere in Styria; he could not tell me where. I only learned from him that a doctor, Ljubojević, often visited her (he is probably the lawyer and landowner in Velika Gorica). I know nothing else. So I'm returning the letter to you—and if I find anything further, I'll let you know.

Always count on me if you need anything. You are a grown-up child, my dear, and you indulge in despair when it is out of place. It would be good for you to come to me for treatment again, as you did when you came from Vienna, remember? In any case: pull yourself together because I don't want to see you like this.

I never come across anything you have written. Have you fallen silent?

With us, everyone is healthy, thank God, and happy. My Đuro (his name is the same as yours, but he won't be such a coward) is already a little man. Anka greets you, and Micika blesses you.

Cheers—and cheer up!

Chapter VII

Toša's answer came when Andrijašević was no longer expecting it. For the first few days, he waited, trying to convince himself that if Toša did what he had begged him to do, his luck would turn around. He no longer thought of going to Zagreb alone; the second month of summer break found him in even worse despair. It seemed wrong to him that he already ran out of money on the first of the month after paying off his debts and settling in advance for his room and board. So he opted out of the board at the rental and ate at the inn.

The summer heat was driving him out of the house anyway. The sun baked the rocks like iron; the nights were not much cooler. During the day, life in town came to a halt; the heavy air was barely breathable. Working did not come easy; to escape the humidity was only possible when bathing; after doing that, it became even more intolerable. People were lethargic, and only during the evening did the town revive a bit.

Since the letter addressed to Vera returned un-opened, Đuro had been wondering what could have

141

happened to the Hrabars. His imagination, always ready to formulate any number of combinations, found plenty to nourish it in this unknown but undoubtedly unpleasant and challenging affair unfolding in Zagreb. All his elucubrations ended in the same way: someone asked for Vera's hand in marriage and the Hrabars were forcing her to accept. She felt too weak to counter the daily onslaught by herself so she called him by telegram for help.

What next? He didn't know the answer to that question, which plagued him.

"Vera didn't get my letter—she didn't even learn that I wrote to her. She was waiting for me—and she didn't wait long enough. What did she do?"

He didn't dare tell himself that she may have given up. It seemed impossible, but he quietly resented her, she who was not burdened by daily responsibilities, for giving up and wiring him. At the same time, he, wretched man that he was, suffered as if imprisoned and had not ceased to love and believe in her.

The constant thought about this secret event in Vera's life made him very irritable. He could not sit still, even for half an hour; he would throw the books down after reading the first pages and spend the rest of the day lying around, killed by the heat, suffocated by his heavy thoughts.

And the letter from Toša, which he was counting on to change everything, did not come.

"He cares nothing for me anymore, either. Everyone has abandoned me; they have left me to die like a fish out of water. What did I write to him?—more about

Vera! He has his hands full caring for his family—how could he also take care of my troubles!"

His fatigue and tedium increased every day. Almost unaware of the change, Andrijašević started to spend most of the day in the tavern, reading the newspaper and—finally—playing cards with the same company that had until recently disgusted him.

"Something has to be done; if I remain alone, I'll fall ill." He had no one to associate with. All conversations with people revolved around the craziest trifles; politics, for which Andrijašević had no passion, was the only thing that pleased this small world. It sometimes led to heated exchanges, but Đuro could not understand why they debated so passionately, so tenaciously, even insulting their opponents and defending their own opinion, which was obviously derived from the platform of one of the parties.

"They spout such big words! They talk about ideals; they enshrine themselves in truth and righteousness yet fail to see that they cannot understand a thing because of the narrowness of their perspectives. They take comfort in these declamations, I'd say... for any more serious intentions in all this are lacking. Maybe they are trying to achieve these far-reaching general goals because they cannot deal with even the smallest, easiest ones for themselves or their immediate surroundings."

Politics and the effort to spend as many evenings in lively company—that did not need to be so lively, as long as they were together—seemed to Andrijašević to be the only distraction, the only entertainment for most of the people around him. And they drank so much that

Andrijašević saw his tab showing progress every day. By the time he returned home late at night, tired from the evening's company, it was easier for him; at least he could sleep late the next day, leaving fewer hours for tedium or struggles with his thoughts.

He managed, in this way, to regain his composure somehow and make his life more tolerable. There were days when he was overcome by despair and disgust—he didn't want to see anyone, hated everybody. His head would ache from his incessant smoking as he lay on the couch and, in vain, sought peace. But after these moments, apathy would again overtake him—and after five or six weeks, it no longer seemed unusual for him to spend all night playing cards for a pittance, listening to well-known and half-known jokes, and drinking.

The people he got to know at the inn compelled him to mingle with almost all the "better society" in the town. At predetermined times of day, he and his crowd strolled along the coast or down the promenade. During these walks, he often ran into Miss Darinka. She told him she hadn't believed in his illness for a moment and was angry at him for not coming on the trip, yet she obviously still enjoyed his company.

After mid-August, Darinka said that the next day she would introduce the doctor to a "beautiful girl" (she always called Đuro "doctor"). That beautiful girl was the daughter of the director of the tobacco factory in the town, a charming young woman just out of boarding school. Darinka praised her as a very clever young lady and finally said to Đuro, jokingly:

"Just don't fall in love with her!"

"Me? You don't know me, Miss," said Andrijašević embarrassed that he answered Darinka's words so seriously, almost with a sigh. The memory of Vera stabbed him through the heart—and he couldn't hide a wince of aggravation.

The carefree Darinka overlooked this and the next day ceremoniously introduced Andrijašević to "her foster child," Miss Minka. Đuro's latest acquaintance seemed neither better nor worse than all the beautiful girls at that age. She put on sentimental airs; she, like Darinka, was always in good spirits and was the only person in town who was unaffected by the heat since she could spend half a day in the water.

Andrijašević grew accustomed to her; the three of them would walk ("I'm Minka's chaperone," Darinka laughed), and twice they took a boat. The company of the young women did not seem of any significant relevance to Andrijašević. Still, just as he would breathe a sigh of relief when he found someone at the inn with whom he could spend the evening, the company of these two merry creatures filled an hour—and that was enough for him.

Sometimes it occurred to him that he might not have felt so badly about the weight of small-town life had he met more people earlier, especially if he had had the pleasure of such walks and conversations with Darinka and Minka or whomever. He once said that Darinka was right when she claimed that in a small town, one must live "according to the menu."

"That's right: *Wiener Mode* publishes a schedule every week for what one can cook each day. We should do the same: plan how we will have fun two or three days in advance. Otherwise, it would be impossible to fill the days, especially in summer. And so you see: we take walks now, then there are evenings, again in winter the occasional dance class—there is always something to do."

And Darinka immediately added that the university students who are now home on holiday were preparing to put on an amateur show.

"Minka and I will participate; don't you want to, Minka? Yes you do, yes you do. And it would be nice if you would too."

Darinka had apparently been entrusted with the mission of asking Andrijašević if he would like the job of directing the amateur troupe.

At first, Đuro refused; but when Darinka told him that she and Minka would have to rehearse every night, he thought it is wiser to agree.

*

So it was that he joined the student group. Ready as always to find in everything that happened to him a good or bad sign, Andrijašević went to work with those involved in the student theatrical, with a love that surprised even him. The youths saw in him a respected writer and a man "whose name was famous," and he was happy to have them listening to him. He enjoyed their belief in a future that was not based on great words or a distant reality; Đuro could feel it in every exclamation of his young comrades. And their parties were the best, even though the nights were shorter for the students; their conversation was more colorful, richer. Andrijašević was most pleased that he was the center of some, albeit small, action; the conviction of his worth and the respect he enjoyed consoled him and hid the factual emptiness he felt in his soul. It so happened that he rejuvenated himself for a while with these new people who, you may say, had nothing in common with Andrijašević's previous acquaintances. The young men made dinner for a lark, and invited the young women who were taking part. The dinner went wonderfully; Đuro began to feel that all life's problems, his service and other worries could be endured if it weren't for his troubles with Vera.

The chaperones for the young ladies were also at the dinner. This is how Đuro met Minka's mother and was invited for a visit.

The factory director's house belonged to the town's elite. Andrijašević was surprised by its luxury, which he had not seen anywhere else. He was received most kindly—so it was especially hard for him to use the appropriate tone of voice. But Darinka smoothed everything out with her laughter—and the afternoon went by quickly, even too quickly. Minka tried her hand at the piano—and Đuro was prevailed upon to play with her. But already after the first notes, Minka protested that she could play no longer, saying she was ashamed at being—"such a bungler," playing with him, a "virtuoso."

Finally, Đuro had to play a solo piece. At first, his fingers strained to obey him—but very soon, he completely overcame his insecurity born of a prolonged lack of practice and he launched vigorously into his favorite Grieg piece.

Praise followed, applause, and—again, Darinka's reproaches that such a "lovely man" as himself was so neglectful and did nothing to enhance the town's social life.

The preparations for the performance itself took up a whole week after that. Andrijašević came to life: haste and rehearsals made him tired and sleep well at night; the next day he felt fresher and calmer.

But the performance itself ended quite unexpectedly. Just before the evening when the long-rehearsed production was to be put on, an invitation appeared in the Zagreb daily newspapers from a student organization, petitioning colleagues to join a cooperative that would "popularize culture." Among the books to be published, two or three popular leaflets by German *Freethinkers* shared first place. Under the invitation were signatures, including several by the organizers of the performance.

A whole storm ensued. The opposition's broadsheet condemned these "young and feckless folks who are bent on undermining the very foundations of our entire past, present, and future."

In the second issue, there was already someone from Senj highlighting the signatures of local students, accusing them of treason, indifference to politics, and even perfidy, because "while they are signing such treacherous calls to pave the way—under the guise of freedom of thought among the people—for the rampages of the Freemasons and all other enemies of our anguished homeland, here in Senj they organize performances for the benefit of a student support group and do not hesitate to invite the clergy and the rest of the community who object to giving credence to these 'robin redbreasts and fledglings' who know not what they do." And at the end of the letter, there were several clear allusions to Đuro: "one of the people who should have had the education of the youth at heart"—"a man who has shown throughout his life that he is in no way bound to the interests of the town and homeland where he lives"—"allegedly a writer"—"supposedly a metropolitan snob" who thinks he is allowed to "toy with the feelings of his fellow citizens."

It continued in the same tone. The letter caused a revolution in the town: meetings were held, gossiping ensued, Andrijašević received two or three letters of sympathy, a few pieces of advice, and the question: "What will he do in response." One portion of the citizenry returned their invitations to the performance—and within three days, there were two factions poised and fully established—one for, the other against.

Andrijašević was disgusted.

"Good God, what wrongs have I done to them? And in general, what does the petition have to do with me and this harmless show?"

"No, they will not allow me to advance. All you want is to cheer up a little, come to life—but they don't let you. Shut up and grit your teeth, bite your tongue and stagger ever onward."

"So even this is out of bounds! As if I cared; if it hadn't been for Darinka, I never would have considered joining the student society."

He wanted to put everything behind him, to tell everyone how silly and pointless this was, and to retreat
again to his corner. But retreat was no longer possible.
Passions seethed; Andrijašević was surrounded by people he had never had contact with before who urged
him "not to give in." "It must be shown that we don't
have to obey anyone's orders." The students, the organizers of the production, were the most belligerent—and
Đura's sour mood didn't help.

"Now, we must see our plan through; the performance will be held and it will succeed; and as to 'them,' let
them rant and rave!"

Due to the fracas, very few people came, so there
was no dance after midnight. Those who remained gathered at the tavern—where a makeshift assembly con-
vened with speeches.

Andrijašević sat, abashed and despondent, with Darinka
and Minka, trying in vain to recover his good mood. When
they toasted him as "one of the most advanced of our
writers who even under these circumstances did not hide
his conviction," he almost started laughing.

"In a small world like this, everything assumes the
meaning of something big. They are declaring me! me!
some sort of political agitator!"

The next day he woke up with a headache and bitterness in his soul. He was pulled out of bed by Gračar,
who had just returned from a vacation and learned while
in Zagreb that it was Žuvić who had written the letter
against him.

"To tell you the truth, I do not care; I enter all this
like Pilate entered the Creed."

"You shouldn't have kept quiet. You can laugh as I laugh: but you shouldn't have given them the satisfaction of bragging about how you didn't dare send a correction."

"What was there for me to correct, man! Am I to spar like Don Quixote with windmills?"

"Windmills or not, they will reap riches from this. You will see how he will lie to Headmaster Maričić, who was in charge over the holidays in his stead. Maričić also undoubtedly had a hand in the letter, so he will describe you as the blackest devil. But up you get—let's go for a beer; during my two days in Zagreb, I learned to drink beer before noon."

*

At first, the affair with school production hurt and angered Andrijašević. Later, remembering the suggestions from some people not to give in, the students' toasts that evening, the spat between the two factions that formed in town—everything took on a tragicomic air. He began to be amused by those who were for the performance and those who were against it—and in the end, he resolved to ridicule it all. He went out and bought writing paper (he could not write on plain paper or in school notebooks where he usually jotted his notes while studying because, for literary work, he needed especially fine material) and wrote in capital letters the title *War in Ždrenje, a comedy*. The characters readily took their places on stage; as to the plot, all he had to do was copy the event as it had unfolded. At the center of the comedy is a person who, without even knowing why, becomes the hero of the day in a small town, the site of a battle between frogs and mice.

Surprisingly, his work progressed well. Re-reading the first act, he liked how sharply, with outrage and ridicule, he'd outlined the main characters. Žuvić and Maričić were also sketched; the sympathetic faction was mainly represented by Darinka and then the protagonist of the comedy.

But further work did not go as easily. Andrijašević, tightening the knot, became entangled in it himself; and by the third act he had completely lost the irony. The hero became increasingly lackluster: the comedy turned into a woeful picture of provincial life, which made the hero nervous, it was too serious, and finally brought him into such a bind that he could not find a harmonious ending.

As always, he worked on this for several days, productively, with no thought of anything else, and the manuscript sheets piled up; after a night of writing (he could never write during the day), he woke up in the morning with a headache.

In the third act, the high point of the comedy is a move to form a faction headed by Bratanić, the main character. But at a meeting to establish a new society 'for the revival of the town of Ždrenje,' Bratanić reveals to his associates and friends how ridiculous their struggle is. The assembly disperses amid the hoots and catcalls of like-minded people who move off stage and leave Bratanić alone with a single friend. What follows is a conversation about small-town life; in this, the comedy deviates entirely from its original course: Bratanić and his friend complain to each other, criticize and swear, no longer with laughter, indeed almost in tears.

When he finished that act, Đuro read his work. The further he read, the more his brow darkened—at the end, he was utterly desolate.

"That's me, myself! That's why what was a joke became reality; and the struggle between the frogs and the mice became the struggle of the hawks around my chest! These are my thoughts and my misery—ah, it's all even sadder when I see it written and acted by actual characters."

He could no longer write. He knew he had no strength to finish; the ending would have to be ugly— the hero's demise. And somehow, he was fearful of writing that prophecy for himself—so the War in Ždrenje remained in a drawer, unfinished, and his mockery of the provincials turned into resignation and sluggish vegetating.

*

Toša's answer found him in this mood. He couldn't read the lines calmly; he jumped from one paragraph to the next to grasp the letter's gist in a second.

"Nothing—nothing. Toša didn't see her; he didn't tell her anything." His letter, enclosed in Toša's envelope, looked at him so sadly, as if malicious.

"She's ill—poor thing. So we are in the same boat! I'm rotting and decaying here—and she is ill."

He wondered where they could have gone. In the past, they had gone on holiday to stay with relatives in Gorski Kotar.

"To Styria? Where in Styria? I am sure they are in a village so far away that I could never find her."

He also opened his letter and read the long description of his troubles intended for Vera. Despair peeked from every line—despair without hope. He read the last lines ... "Don't leave me! Everything can still be as it should be: I will suffer, wrest my soul asunder—but I must know that you love me and are mine. I have no one else, my mother has become alien to me, she has moved into a world to me completely unknown, I have no siblings, I do not have a friend, if I lose you, I shall end it all."

"But you won't, will you? No, Vera, don't—ah, why do I even ask you that. I can see from your telegram that you are and will remain mine. Be patient, child, do your best to resist—and I'll do the same even if doing so is agony. But this cannot last forever—that would be too awful. We have wronged no one; we shall not be punished without mercy. Have courage—and wait for me!"

"Yes, this is what I wrote then—My God, look at the impact of words! Words can cast a spell; they can make you lie to yourself. How will this waiting end? By becoming a Gračar—with the shame of all those unpaid debts?"

For the first time, he thought of death. The fact that Vera could have died did not seem so terrible. He imagined her laid out in a casket, pale, blessed among the candles. And he transformed his grief for her in his imagination, as if she really had died. His grief was not desperate: quietly, calmly, he gazed at the black veil covering her face, untouched by anyone else's hand ... "I will follow you soon, my child...."

After imagining Vera's death, he viewed his imaginary future life quite differently. He would be calm—and wait for the moment of meeting her in the endless peace of the darkness of the afterlife. At that moment, he was not upset by anyone's beliefs that the life of the soul ceases when the life of the organism does: mystical, almost religious joy suffused him, thinking he was with her, in equal yet not gnawing pain ...

With this image in mind, he found himself on the road below the Nehaj fortress walls. The day was Sunday—and the town was quiet, without the bustle of traffic and no boats were out on the water. A storm was clearly brewing; the Vratnik Pass was enveloped in a dark cap, while the rest of the sky was blanketed not by clouds but by a solid, ash-gray cloak. The sea spread, calm, all the way to its edges along the islands, endlessly disappearing into almost the very same leaden hue of packed dirt.

... There is peace here ... and the fish cannot talk—the sea is silent and buries everything. What is sleeping the eternal dream beneath its surface? How many people, how many things lie buried there, without fear of ever coming to the surface, to life! And death must be just as quiet."

Deep somewhere, inaudibly, in the furthest corner of his soul, the thought came to him of how nice and comfortable it would be to rest under the cover of this vast, unrippling surface.

Chapter VIII

The empty school building returned to life. The students gathered on their first visit to the church to invoke God's help for the new school year. In the atrium, one could hear many voices; the meeting of colleagues after the holidays, the enrollment of new students, and the distribution of timesheets and exam schedules gave many reasons for hurry, discussions, writing and running through the hallways.

Andrijašević was spent, groggy from a sleepless night; he sat in the classroom by his desk while entering the students' names in the new registers. Rajčić, sitting opposite him, repeated each name aloud and took note of his remarks. Đuro seemed to be busy and engrossed in his work; he did not want to look at Maričić, who the day before had submitted to the headmaster his report on the events over the holidays; he replied to Žuvic's greetings by turning his head. It was apparent that a few of the folks gathered in the room were not happy to meet the others, hence they spoke too loudly and trotted about, trying to cover up the conflicts.

The headmaster entered and greeted everyone courteously, as always, with "dear colleague"; he praised

Gračar for gaining weight, congratulated Žuvić on his promotion, and told Rajčić that the authorities were satisfied with his latest textbook revision. He stopped and asked Andrijašević how he spent the holidays.

"Thank you, as well as possible."

"I know, I know—you must have a lot to study for your exam. And you had fun, as I hear, organizing other activities..."

Đuro thought these words were supposed to be the beginning of a more extended conversation, so he didn't answer.

At that moment, in came Lukačevski, fresh and cheerful, wearing a new suit. Against his custom, he greeted everyone in a lively tone, exchanged a few words with the headmaster, and immediately addressed Đuro.

"I was away from here, my friend—ah, I feel completely refreshed."

And he started talking about experiences from a journey that had gone no further than Graz and Vienna but was, for Lukačevski, like a world tour.

"And you?"

"The usual tedium."

"Now, now—I was told you became a real hero of the day. I have also heard of your visits to the director of the factory; splendid, splendid."

"What does he mean by that?" thought Đuro.

The bell rang; it was time to get ready for church.

Andrijašević mechanically stood next to his last year's class, without thinking that it had not yet been decided who would be the teacher for each classroom this year.

Lukačevski immediately came over and walked him to church.

"You are standing by your last year's students; I don't think he'll give them to you this year."

"I do not care."

"They won't give you others either, I guess. They've had it with you."

"Me? Who?"

"All of them. You know they were ready to go to the bishop to have him intercede with the authorities against you. You were not cautious. The tale with the student performance was over the top."

"Talking about this is stupid; I had nothing to do with the whole thing."

"How come? Maričić told the headmaster that you were the students' leader and that they even toasted to you."

"It was like this: Miss Darinka asked me to accept the management of an amateur show and ..."

Đuro briefly related what had happened.

"Miss Darinka did you no favors. In general, she behaves far too freely with these people. Under the current circumstances, one should take great care of oneself."

"I see no alliance between Miss Darinka's behavior and Maričić's gossiping."

"Anyway, beware of her!"

"Now, please!" Andrijašević laughed, "unless you have more to say about your travels, we needn't talk any further."

Lukačevski needed no prompting to go on about his holidays; he immediately shook out a hundred impressions and experiences. Đuro grew tired of his stories; he was hungover and irked by Lukačevski's cheerful mood, his sharp observations, and especially the satisfaction radiating from his every word.

"He talks as if I have never been beyond Rijeka. Is this self-promotion or just his desire to infuriate me?"

It was neither; Lukačevski was simply happy to tell stories about events in a real city. But his words unintentionally hurt Đuro—he was relieved once they reached the church.

The young people lined up; the younger ones stood with their classes and the older ones took seats. In the back, there were two empty benches left for the teachers; but Đuro noticed he would have to sit next to Žuvić (the others had already settled in), so he leaned against the stonewall, moving to a shadowy corner away from his colleagues.

Not much light penetrated the ancient church, once belonging to friars. Silent and condensed, its cool air gave the illusion of another world, unlike the beautiful day outdoors. The bell rang, the organ played, and the service began. The children's voices joined into a chorus, imperfect and a little dissonant. Still, their unison perfectly matched the unadorned pillars, the timeworn tombstones of Senj's nobles and bishops, the whispers of pious women, and the dim light of the soaring empty space.

In recent times, Andrijašević had often thought about the consolation of faith. As an artist and a soul with elevated feelings, he enjoyed the mystique of religious services, the priests' ceremonious movements, and the severity of the sacred music. But he could never understand the connection between faith and life; scientific belief spoke against the ethical side, and yet it did not acknowledge that religion may indeed bring peace to the soul. For the common man, with rough and simple feelings—so he reasoned—faith can be a great deal and everything; but I, a philosopher, what should I ask of a deity who cannot alter the course of predetermined events? What can I promise when my will is subject to laws which I do not know and are beyond my control?

There was not a trace of aggressiveness in him nor a spark of desire to fend off religious feelings or steal them from anyone. He didn't think it interesting that there were people in the same small-town society who liked to be called "free thinkers" even when they had no thoughts whatsoever. Yet the world of the church was foreign to him. Even now, during the service, he was interested in every little detail; he saw something beautiful and majestic in the holy bloodless sacrifice that is renewed every day—but his hands did not fold in prayer, nor did the priest speak to his heart.

Surprisingly, and to the mild displeasure of the children who were expecting only a "short Mass," it turned out that, contrary to custom, the gymnasium religious teacher would be holding a sermon. Đuro couldn't stand this for long: the spoken word, the instructions on how to live your life irritated him, as if someone had interrupted a lyric poem by skipping a strophe and continuing on in prose. But from the first words, he saw that today's sermon would be unique, without the usual advice about school and children's errors. The religion teacher ascended to the pulpit and first apologized for giving a sermon on this day, which is usually dedicated only to invoking the Holy Spirit.

"But, dear disciples, the circumstances are so serious that I must break with custom. A roaring lion roams amongst you ... and lurks on your souls, the *Leo rugiens*, as the Scriptures say..."

After his fifth or sixth sentence, what the preacher was aiming for with his talk became clear. He held forth about how the devil used young hearts to spew his damned seed, seduced young men to serve him, and forced them to lure others into his service. "He will trick you, my disciples, and this is why I, your spiritual father, must warn you of this threatening peril."

These words were followed by the story of the students' petition in Zagreb, which caused the problems with the performance. Andrijašević began listening carefully. The religion teacher spoke cautiously, in general, but there were many sentences in which Đuro espied an attack against himself. The preacher made no mention of the play, but he declared to the young people two or three times that "regrettably, this plague from the west has come to our ageold town." Two or three colleagues inadvertently swiveled to look at Andrijašević, and he noticed the glances of several of the older students.

"Et tu, Brute! I always got along well with him; I never hurt him. He considers me an enemy—and what can I do!—I cannot wash it away."

For a moment, Đuro listened as if this wasn't about him at all.

"My colleague ought to have been more careful. The students surely understand this. All too well. Our relationship will become impossible."

Glances were shooting at him from many sides (it may not have been so, but he convinced himself that some of the other devout were also watching him); staying became awkward. He retreated even more deeply into shadow, and when the priest finished, he left.

*

He found Darinka and Minka on the promenade. They immediately noticed that he was upset and asked why.

"Ah, more nonsense." Đuro told them about what had happened in the church.

"They've really thrown themselves at you! Mind-numbing people! Instead of being glad to have you here among us."

Minka echoed Darinka's words. Andrijašević thought Minka's words and the look in her eyes were sincere and that she regretted his latest misfortune.

"You needn't feel so sorry for me. It only upset me for a moment."

(The hero in Ždrenje–the sarcasm buzzed in his heart)

"You know what?" continued Darinka. "Why don't we take a stroll along the promenade and hear what they're saying."

But Đuro did not like the idea. He did, however, promise to visit Minka for afternoon tea.

"We will enjoy ourselves, and let them say what they want!" said Darinka with a tone of defiance that suited her perfectly. It's best not to get tangled up in this at all. Come to our house and don't worry about the others.

"I, too, can see that this company is not having a good effect on me."

"Well, last year, you were friends with that Lukačevski—and he is the worst of them all. An egoist, he curses everybody—and he is a coward; you'll see that he won't stand up for you when the time comes."

"You are so harsh in your judgment of him. Tit for tat. He doesn't seem to like you either."

"What—Has he said anything about me?"

"No, no," Đuro denied Darinka's suspicion. "I just noticed he doesn't like you very much."

"It used to be different," replied Darinka in anger. "Lukačevski proposed to me—did you know that? I spurned him; I don't like men who are calculating and selfish."

"Ha-ha-ha!" laughed Andrijašević to himself, but his internal laughter nearly rose to his lips. "My cold, sovereign Lukačevski! Everything about him is artificial—all buried away because of spurned love. And he held forth with those long moral sermons that teachers should never marry. A scalded sage! Comical!"

He liked what he'd heard about Lukačevski. As if he had found an excuse and some relief in unmasking Lukačevski's composure.

That afternoon at Minka's, the conversation mainly revolved around the sermon. The factory director consoled the "Doctor."

"They don't work at a proper job, so they toy with minutiae. They produce nothing. If they were engaged in genuine work producing something real—like rolling leaves into cigars to sell later—you'd see that this sort of meddlesome behavior wouldn't occur to them."

Andrijašević stayed on for dinner, during which the director's wife behaved in such a way that Đuro was taken aback by how well they treated him.

After ten, he left to return to his rooms. Passing by the inn, through the window he noticed the silhouette of Lukačevski sitting at a table; he couldn't help but go in.

"He'll be none too pleased when I tell him my explanation for all his talk about his firm principles. A spurned proposal of marriage—the whole mystery in a nutshell!"

But next to Lukačevski, to Andrijašević's great surprise, sat the headmaster.

"Oh, you are showing up late today, my colleague Lukačevski told me. We thought you wouldn't come. And I was waiting here for you."

"The headmaster was talking with me about what happened today," explained Lukačevski.

"Dear colleague, would you mind if I take an hour of your time? I believe we can talk about this in front of our colleague Lukačevski," the headmaster said rather ceremoniously, lowering his voice.

"Be my guest."

"In short, to get to the point. Of course, I'm not talking to you as your superior—hence why I chose to come here—but as a colleague and a friend, I'm asking you what you intend to do after the ... how should I put it— incident at church today?"

The waitress came over to Đuro to ask what he wanted.

"A glass of beer."

"It's not as easy as you might think, particularly not for me." The headmaster slowly pulled out and opened his box of wax matches. "Will you take any steps?"

"I'm sorry, but I don't quite understand what you mean. What steps could I or should I take?"

"I will not gainsay—I repeat—I will not gainsay that the religion teacher erred. One can warn young people against these dangers without casting aspersions. Yes, I do not mean to gainsay it—and rest assured, I will not hesitate to do everything I can to prevent similar incidents from happening again. I desire peace in the institution, collegiality among colleagues, and harmony between our young people and their teachers. In no way will I allow this harmony to be jeopardized, to harm—maybe even with no ill intentions—the excellent reputation the institution enjoys. As to that, you may be rest assured. But as to you, again, I wish to be sure that you will not do anything that might cause complications."

"Mr. Headmaster, Sir, please forgive me again, but I am unclear as to what you want from me."

"I want nothing and will ask for nothing from you, my friend," the words came slowly out of the headmaster's mouth, as if he were reading them from a book, spelling them out letter by letter), but merely as your colleague in the same profession and as a man who holds all teachers in his heart, please promise me that you will not take any steps without my knowledge.

"And what might these steps be?"

"I heard today that you mean to complain to the authorities."

"That is ridiculous; today, I haven't spoken to anyone about this; I spent all afternoon at the home of the director of the factory."

Lukačevski laughed faintly.

"What's so funny?" – Andrijašević turned to him nervously.

"Nothing, nothing—I was thinking about how people fabricate things so readily..."

"There is no need to stray from our most crucial point. If you haven't spoken with anyone, so much the better. And I, as a friend, ask you not to do anything in the future without consulting me."

"I can promise you that right now. To me, the whole thing is just plain silly. I never had anything to do with the student movement nor did I mean to demonstrate against anyone by organizing the performance. If people made a mountain out of this, too bad for them. It's too ludicrous for me to tear my hair out."

"The matter may be a bit more serious; there is dissatisfaction among the townspeople—against you. We must not have a negative impact; we are guests in this town daily, today and tomorrow."

("Ugh, oh if only now were already tomorrow!" sighed Andrijašević to himself.)

The headmaster stopped and lit his cigar.

"As things now stand, there is no danger of tangling ourselves in an intricate web that would be impossible to unravel later without harming those involved. But, the conflict may intensify, let's say—let's say," the headmaster looked straight at Đuro, "should there be an article or a letter to the newspaper..."

"It is not in my nature to write anonymous letters. And newspapers have more important work to do than to dwell on these trivialities."

"I like that, bravo, bravo." The headmaster pronounced this Bra-avo, bra-avo. "So I can be sure that this incident will end for you in amity? Thank you, my sincere thanks. You have put my worries to rest; it will be a great credit to you if our institute's good name is not brought into question."

Andrijašević followed the headmaster's words with real pleasure: "He acts as if he were on stage! It would be a shame not to write about this!"

Lukačevski remained quiet and did not intervene. "Is it contempt or fear?" thought Đuro. "If one believes Darinka, Lukačevski is afraid to show he agrees with me openly."

"They're so funny, so very funny. This is worth describing, bringing it all out in the open, deriding them from the heart, and brandishing my weapons simultaneously."

The next day he sat at his desk and wrote the fourth act of his comedy. The title *War in Ždrenje* seemed too weak; so he wrote in capital letters, deliberately, on the first sheet *Revolution in Ždrenje*, a comedy in four acts by Đuro Andrijašević.

*

For three days, people were talking only about the sermon. Everyone greeted Andrijašević with a forced cordiality; being in school with colleagues became impossible, so Đuro came in only to teach his classes and left the building immediately after, without speaking with anyone.

Everything infuriated him. Rajčić spoke of their friendship with comic pathos, saying how he would show "them" (he didn't get along with the teacher of religion). Remoli, a merchant of Italian descent who was angry with Maričić, "that Jesuit," hurried to express his condolences to Andrijašević while at the same time putting in a good word for his son, a well-known scoundrel. Đuro was particularly annoyed by Tramovac, a retired teacher. His boy had been expelled from boarding school the year before, and ever since then Tramovac had hated the bishop (who, of course, had nothing to do with it); he moved to Senj, where he could not go hunting as often as he liked, this being the only activity he truly enjoyed. Tramovac came looking twice for Đuro at his apartment and talked about how "all the freer elements, all the people who know we lived in the 20th century should organize to defend themselves against the 'Pope's tyranny' from which the teachers had only barely freed the school but which now was intent on destroying teachers and professors alike." Andrijašević could hardly get rid of him; he was disgusted by the ridiculous speech and the insolence with which the man spoke of the profession (as far as being an educator, he had raised his child quite disgracefully!).

There were no classes on Thursday. Đuro received a call from Minka's parents and went to visit them. The day was beautiful, so they wanted to show him an

American game set on the lawn of the director's garden consisting of propelling a ball over the ground through iron hoops. In the middle of the outing, the gymnasium janitor brought him a message from the headmaster asking to see him immediately if possible.

"This is too much, being summoned from here," he thought and refused. But the others guessed that the headmaster wanted to speak with him about something important and pressed him to go; it won't last long, and it's nearby, so we don't mind waiting a few hours.

The headmaster was pacing around his room with big steps and had his back to the door as Đuro entered.

"Good thing you responded immediately. What I have to tell you is of the utmost importance."

Apparently, the headmaster was upset. He forgot his usual poses and forgot to offer Đuro a seat. He went to his desk and picked up the *Nova misao* newspaper lying on the table.

"When I spoke to you on Sunday night, I thought we were talking like serious people who know what they say and what they promise." His sharp tone struck Đuro, who was angry at being summoned in the middle of a quiet afternoon, and now he had to listen to this tone!

"Please kindly refrain from such moral remarks. I know what I was saying then, and I always know what I am doing."

"So my way of speaking seems too direct, does it? I'm surprised that it surprises you. After this," the headmaster handed him *Nova misao* issue, "I don't believe you have the right to resent my bluntness."

"After what? What?"

170

"How—after what? Who are you pretending to be?"

Đuro picked up the newspaper mechanically and noticed red ink scribbled all over an article on the first page. The latest scandal in the church. He read a few lines and realized it was describing the sermon and an attack on a teacher of religion, reactionaries, ultramontanism, gravediggers of liberty, and so forth—in a familiar tone.

"Who wrote this, please?"

"I have no idea."

"Am I mistaken in thinking you reported this or someone close to you did?"

"Please don't raise your voice. I did not write this—nor do I know who did." Đuro blushed and felt the blood rush to his head. "I've had enough of this nonsense. You summon me here to tell me about a letter I neither know nor care about."

"I called you in as your superior ...," (the headmaster recited a whole litany of official instructions about his duties).

"That's all fine; but I repeat that I have nothing to do with anonymous letters and do not know what to say about it. I have other things to attend to. Respectfully I take my leave!"

The headmaster stood there with his mouth open. He couldn't decide whether to call Đuro back or to assume the role of the injured party and chase after him. He could see that Andrijašević had truly known nothing about the letter, and this especially angered him.

"He's telling the truth; otherwise, he wouldn't have dared leave me like this and avoid listening to his superior!"

The janitor received three reprimands that same afternoon.

*

His day was ruined. Đuro returned to Minka's, but the earlier enjoyment was gone. Nervous and restless, he tried with all his might to control himself—and this nearly brought on a headache.

Darinka and the others guessed something must have happened but didn't dare ask. There was no way to revive the party; at his first opportunity, Đuro decided to leave.

"I am spoiling the good spirits of others! Wherever I go, I ruin the mood."

In the evening, as he was getting ready to go out to the inn, Tramovac came to him.

"I chose not to come during the day because I would rather not be seen with you. We must be cautious; the enemy is strong."

Beyond endless phrases borrowed from the liberal newspapers, he showed Đuro a broadsheet, on which they were encouraged to enroll as members in the new "liberal reading room." There were no names yet on the sheet.

"Why not sign it yourself?"

"I ... I can't be the first. The thing primarily came about because of you; you are a teacher; the director of the factory and Remoli, the merchant, are your friends; three such respectable persons, so let them be first, and then we can sign on after them. As you know, there are all sorts of people—it's best to be cautious; I have a son in the gymnasium. Later, when the matter is made public, I, too, will sign."

"Take it back ..."

"What? You don't dare? Ah, the headmaster must have scared you. Fear not; many of us are disgruntled. We are confident of the sympathies of all Croatian teachers. And while I didn't sign, don't think I don't do my part: I do more than others. I'll tell you," (there were only the two of them in the room, but the teacher was still whispering), "to stay among us—did you read the letter in *Nova misao*? And? Did I spice it up for them well?"

"Get away from me, please. I don't want to know anything; leave me alone."

"But please, you as a progressive man..."

"Go away! I don't want to hear anything more from you! ..." Andrijašević was shaken; he thought about wielding his walking stick.

"But listen! I didn't expect this. I stood up for you in public, yet you..."

"Out! At once! This minute!"

Đuro raised his stick and showed the way to the door. The pensioner turned pale and backed away.

"I'm crazy, completely crazy even to be arguing with him!" Andrijašević was immediately ashamed; he was the first to walk out of the room, leaving the teacher, fearful and alarmed, to pick the rejected pages up off the floor.

Chapter IX

Let's read a few more.

"This one sounds even worse. Listen: 'A new piece by one of the better known among our young novelists was presented yesterday on our stage by its writer.' I don't know, for God's sake, what this genius wanted to say."

"No comments; just read, please, Jagan," Andrijašević said nervously.

"Well ... he writes: 'It is evident that the *Revolution in Ždrenje* was the work of a narrator who lacks a sense of drama.' Oof, that one may hit you hard! ... Don't be angry; I'll go on. 'The comedy has minimal plot and few twists; even if it did, the author didn't know how to resolve it.'"

"Who's signed?"

"Nobody, as usual with our critics. But this fellow has a style worthy of middle school. 'Particularly annoying is that the author's language is not the purest, for example' ..."

"Stop it, no further. Throw it back onto the pile. Take another."

Jagan, Đuro' s latest friend, a colleague who had recently transferred to Senj, sighed and retrieved yet another newspaper. At Đuro's wish, he had written to Zagreb asking his relatives to buy all the papers the day after the premiere of Andrijašević's play; this is then what he'd brought to his friend to read, one after another.

"This one has nothing at all—aha, there are a few lines in the corner. 'The Andrijašević *Revolution in Ždrenje* is a social comedy modeled upon Nestroy's famous piece *Revolution im Krähwinkel.*'"

"Whose play?" asked Andrijašević from the bed where he lazed, smoking.

"Nestroy's: *Revolution im Krähwinkel,* says your critic."

"Never heard of him. Alas."

"'But Nestroy knew how to handle his material much better; although there are many similarities between these plays, our present author did not rise to the level of his Viennese model.'"

"Fool! I didn't even know this Nestroy clown existed."

"'Particularly striking is the similarity in episodic characters.' Well, that is really too idiotic. When you read the *Revolution* to me, I immediately recognized the inspiration in the headmaster and Maričić; this fellow speaks of a resemblance to some farce from the past century. Let's stop here, I'm not going to bother anymore."

"Just one more, please, what does *Preporod* say?"

"So you want to know what the freethinkers say? Where is it... here. So: 'Croatian Theater. The *Revolution in Ždrenje*, a four-act comedy by Đuro Andrijašević. Had this thing been presented before Derenčin's famous satires, it would have been called very good.'—This is the stupidest of all! So what was good last year is no good this year! Let them go; these are the jottings of an unsung playwright, begrudging your success. Your clique is everything, my Đuro, and you're far from Zagreb. If you were up there, some would curse you, others would praise you; this is how everyone wants to parade their wisdom before the fellow from the provinces."

Đuro rose to his feet.

"In any case, I failed and failed. Yet the administration sent me a telegram yesterday saying I had had some success."

"You're naive. With us, all plays succeed the same way. The playwright needs to be there in the theater; students applaud every new thing to come out by a local writer. He is expected to stay sitting in the corner of his box. The applause swells—and if he shows his face, better yet: they call him out again and again just to get a look at him. The final result: two performances even if what you'd written were the new Hamlet. For you let this suffice; you had a good laugh at all the local swamp frogs, and beyond that, who cares!"

But Đuro didn't find it easy to calm down. He saw his work hadn't impressed the audience as much as he'd hoped it might. Before sending the play to Zagreb, he had reread it several times; but every time, it sounded different. One day he thought it was good, the next day, it was bad. The same scene felt first alive to him and well, later, trite. In fact, Jagan persuaded him to bring it to the stage, mostly because he liked the idea that there would be people upset after discovering that they were portrayed in the play.

But—the *Revolution in Ždrenje* was not understood. Đuro felt this was his fault. "I was too focused on my character; I identified with the hero and was no longer an objective judge of the hero's actions. So, in the end, he came across as a hero with a sad face, though I wanted him to make fun of everyone. Unquestionably, I no longer know how to write. Let's stop doing it; there is no longer any point."

He also reported his displeasure to Jagan, but the latter quickly found a silver lining.

"All that matters in the world is pleasing yourself. For your literary work, you received an honorarium; that's enough! We'll drink to it and we will not care!"

But Jagan's point of view did not make Đuro any happier. In one newspaper, he came across a review that sounded quite right to him but was, for that reason, even more harsh and damaging. The same thoughts came to him when he reread his work: that it was not new, that it had turned into the author's lyrical confession, that it portrayed pain but meant to convey irony— all this was clearly spelled out in the article.

He was also convinced of his failure by another fact: *The Revolution in Ždrenje* was not put on again after the first performance. There was nothing new in that, but it hurt that his work did not excite the public and that the characters in the comedy were not striking or powerful enough to hold attention.

He was almost sorry that he'd had the comedy printed. The printed version came out after the first performance; Đuro felt almost ashamed that his name, Đuro Andrijašević, appeared below the title.

Lately, he'd started finding Lukačevski disgusting. From the moment Đuro clashed with the headmaster, he noticed that Lukačevski was no longer using a confidential tone when talking to him about the school and colleagues.

"You are too hot-blooded—you don't know how to handle this," Lukačevski told him, fearing that Đuro's hot blood would at some point cause problems. True, he was still critical of 'provincial problems' and was constantly berating the community. He was dissatisfied with his job and his position in society. Andrijašević started to be offended by the constant cussing; when Lukačevski mentioned 'our general misery,' he was talking about Đuro. It happened twice that they had a serious row; afterward, they ignored one another for several days. In particular, Đuro was upset that Lukačevski publicly condemned his play, "not because it is not good, but because this is no way to exact revenge: washing your dirty laundry on stage."

Andrijašević distanced himself from his friend and used every opportunity to avoid eating at the usual inn.

The only person who was genuinely pleased with Đuro's comedy was Darinka. She drowned in pleasure as "our Doctor" (as Minka and she now called him) excelled in describing some very well known individuals. But the happy hours that Andrijašević spent with her (she did her best to persuade him that *Revolution in Ždrenje* should be performed in Senj the next winter) did not last for long; she could not overcome Đuro's depression, which tormented him twice as much as his literary failure had.

"Powerless, forgotten, an utter failure"—these words kept haunting him.

Furthermore, it so happened that for two weeks he couldn't speak with anyone. *Revolution in Ždrenje* provoked a surge of outrage in the city. Even the more serious of the townspeople, who stood aside and did not interfere in the spats between the factions, did not approve that an outsider had so ridiculed the place where he was living. No one was prepared to understand that for Đuro the choice of the town where he was currently serving had been purely one of happenstance; the setting could just as well have been any other town. What insulted them the most was the similarity between the names of the town in the play, Ždrenj, and their town, Senj. However, just as Đuro described in his comedy, those who had been affected and targeted by the play wanted to pay him back in kind. Some of the lines from the comedy became part of the general parlance; for example, Maričić was referred to by his students using the name of character who portrayed him. This greatly intensified the hatred for the writer; they took their revenge by preaching a proper boycott against him. Đuro had recently noticed that some people no longer greeted him, while others avoided him altogether; he received a few anonymous letters where they scoffed at him and his "disgrace on stage." They spied on him and stalked him, and in the newspapers there were frequent reports of "teachers who carouse and then caricature the very town that feeds them," and so forth.

So, finally, of all those he had gotten to know, the only ones to take his side were Minka's circle (the director's family didn't change in their attitude toward him even for a moment, indeed they were even friendlier) and his two new acquaintances: Jagan and Milošević.

*

Milošević came on board only later, when he realized he could not find other people to cozy up to. Đuro and Jagan met on the first day Jagan arrived in Senj; he had been transferred due to "faults with his job performance" in the middle of the school year and immediately became Đuro's inseparable friend.

Đuro himself did not at first understand what had attracted him so quickly to Jagan, but later on, their overlapping tastes and attitudes made their bond almost intimate. Jagan was four years older than Đuro and looked even older. His exterior was like an old wallet: sturdy, short, paunchy; his short-cropped hair and wispy blond mustache gave his red, rather balding head a distinct look. His pale, watery eyes and puffy cheeks said that Jagan was not engaged in serious business but instead spent most of his time in a tavern.

The tavern was his kingdom. He usually drifted, sleepily, almost timidly down the street as if ashamed of his very shabby suit. But once he was in the tavern—the seedier the better—one could see his inner workings. There he came to life, dispensing jokes and humor. He was an intelligent man, perhaps deeper than one might think at first; he always had witty paradoxes up his sleeve and knew how to defend his opinions with sharp, crushing repartee. But these diatribes were all he knew and liked; he was not concerned about the school; he only read the newspapers when he had no spare change for other enjoyments. Conversation revealed that Jagan had in-depth knowledge of one philosopher or another, this or that scientific theory (even from his own branch of science, geography, which he disliked and mentioned the least). However, the sound of his words showed that Jagan had said the same things many times, that he had imbibed this knowledge and thought about what to say long, long before .

He always sat at the head of the table and was careful that others did not take his place. But that was his only stab at arrogance; otherwise, his character was pliant and decent; and had he not been a hard drinker and accustomed to a disorderly life, one might have easily proclaimed him an exemplar of a creature with no needs whatsoever. He ate little, consumed the simplest meals, and dressed beyond modest. He would give anything for a friend—provided that the friend agreed with his customs at the table, where he did not tolerate contention during toasts. He was not ashamed of his life and his squandered nights, nor did he hide them; indeed he had a particular theory about all this that allowed him to admit frankly to everyone, even the headmaster, that he had been transferred "as punishment" because he had stayed at the table for two days during the celebration of somebody's name day in Gospić.

"I forgot I had classes to run—so there you have it!"

Andrijašević suspected that his friend, at the bottom of his soul, was unhappy and desperate (because otherwise there was no way to explain his indifference to all that could benefit or harm him). Still, Jagan did not display his despair openly, but in his many bittersweet jokes, often ironic but never sentimental. He said he was only sentimental when he was completely drunk, but since he never managed to get completely drunk, he had no chance of being sentimental.

Đuro fell in love with him. He loved his candor, his good heart, and the fact that Jagan hated only two things in the world: hypocrisy and conceit. A few days later, Jagan told him that Lukačevski was a bad man.

"He's not yet as bad as the others."

"He's worse, believe me," said Jagan, crumbling bread (he always did this for fun). "You see: the headmaster is stupid and conceited, but he believes his vocation requires this of him. Lukačevski, on the other hand, suffers from the conceit of cowardice—because he fears revealing who he is."

Jagan did not like Poles at all. He was an upstanding patriot and an upstanding Slav, but he interpreted both in his own way.

"Slavs are, my brother," (his usual turn of phrase) "Russians, your *batushka* is a Slav. Dostoevsky, Lermontov, Pushkin, Saltykov. The Pole is an esthete but knows only the boundaries of Poland. Batushka is a miracle of humanity. Then we, the Croats and Serbs, arrived. And we are not fit for life, same as the Russians. We are Slavs. Those of the Slavs who have mingled with Germans will succeed. The Czechs will not disappear. We will be devoured by the people of Kranj, the Slovenes, and the Serbs by the Bulgarians. This is becoming increasingly clear. The first to fall will be those Croats who are of the purest race. These are the Bosnian Moham-medans. Despite all the impact of religion, these people are pure Slavs. This is why they will disappear."

Jagan would put forth paradoxical and grandiose theories on every topic. It was enough to say something to him to spur a conversation. And all the conversations ended with the same refrain: we are destined to fail, not only as a nation but also each of us as individuals.

"Well, I know I'm failing. I get drunk, I never have a dime, I'm torn, I owe money to every single kind of people. But there is no cure for it. If you want to rein yourself in and break away, you must be strong—and 'kill the old hag,' as Raskolnikov says. You needn't actu-ally murder, but you must conceal your nature, feelings and tastes. You must tell the headmaster he is wise, lie to your colleagues that they are conveyers of culture, and spin children even greater tales. But that's not my job. For the sake of theory, I could teach a subject, say, ethics or history, but dealing with the upbringing of children— how are you going to bring up someone else when you cannot bring up yourself or force yourself to mediocrity and discipline? If you want that for yourself, you will be unhappy, tedious to yourself, empty like Lukačevski, ill like Maričić, and stupid like Žuvić. The best is to let things unfold as they will. Let's see what happens."

"You say this can't end well; Well, my brother, I, too, know that. It would have been even better if those Krauts had not come to power," (Jagan used the worst 'Kraut' to mean 'the very worst') "and invented a new law a year ago. I was a substitute for six years, and I served as they paid me. I was happy, they were happy. And now they want us to take an exam in two years. And I signed the receipt, but I know I will not take the exam."

"So what will you do?"

"There are seven more months until then. Well, even if it were tomorrow, it doesn't matter; I wouldn't crack my head over this. It's best to fail—there. And you know what—we'll still be able to make fifty forints somehow a month. And we will not pay taxes on that as we do now; that immediately gives you one more crown each month;—maybe they'd make me an officer. I was a volunteer."

"You—Jagan—an officer?"

As soon as Jagan felt Đuro objecting to this thought, he stood up for it; defending paradoxes was his only passion.

"And why not? You mean to say there are a lot of Krauts in the army. True. But again, these people have traditions, such as their point of view on duels. They genuinely believe a person has honor that derives from intelligence and societal position. A Jew or our headmaster does not have that belief; they only know profit and the hypocrisy behind this honor."

"So, long live citizen Jagan!"

"Cheers! Long live!" Jagan joined in and was immediately irked that Milošević was not there so they could sing.

Music was the only thing that truly interested him. He did not play an instrument but adored singing and dreamed about concerts and operas. This brought Đuro and him closer to their third friend, Milošević, who came to Senj to serve as town music director after graduating from the Prague Conservatory.

Milošević was not very healthy; he was consumptive. Like all artists, he was quite vain; he found it profoundly offensive that he was forced by penury to accept this disappointing job. He fumed at all the musicians, the students and the church where he had to play the organ—and in the evening, when Ðuro and Jagan came to him, he had only just caught his breath.

The music society had its own rooms (and two more for the Kapellmeister) in an old, empty house outside the town walls. Milošević arranged the space as if he were a student: he had no money for furnishings, so his apartment looked more like a storage room for old instruments, notes, and threadbare suits than a proper home.

The three agreed that, in winter, it is best to light a stove, buy a small barrel of wine and have fun singing and playing music. Milošević was an excellent fiddler, and Ðuro revived his former piano skills. Jagan was their only audience at these "music soirees," But he was far more enthusiastic than an entire theater. They constantly drank, of course—and one or the other would sometimes stay at Milošević's to sleep it off on a pew until the morning.

The "music soirees" increased in frequency, and with them the habit of not returning home before midnight. Jagan was inexhaustible in coming up with new reasons why they needed to drink. And he had a special theory about that, too.

"We have two types of people: one is folks from larger cities and Zagreb, and the other is us, peasants. In Zagreb, when they want to tell an anecdote, in twenty out of a hundred cases, they start like this: 'When I was with that gal ...' We peasants start every memory with the words: 'When we drank at that ...'"

Đuro quickly gave himself over to this way of life. He was happy that he could sleep all day whenever he wasn't teaching; Jagan's company and his "doom theories" gave him peace of mind regarding the many issues that had been bothering him. He even no longer thought often about Vera, though he never admitted this to himself. He considered his love to be something distant, past, nothing but a painful memory.

When *Revolution in Ždrenje* was performed in Zagreb, he woke up for a moment from his daily grogginess and hoped Vera would be happy to hear of his comedy; maybe she would even watch it herself. His hope for success was linked to the premonition that Vera would be there at the theater, rejoicing for him, knowing he was alive, that he had not forgotten her.

The poor reception for the play was therefore all the more devastating. Not for his literary fame, but he felt awful precisely for the sake of Vera.

"She saw my work, read the unfavorable reviews; she knows I can no longer create anything, that I am stripped bare, helpless, ruined."

And then from the depths came a voice telling him it was better this way. "What could I give her after these two years when I have given up looking after myself? I don't even care if my shirt is clean... We just drink... Jagan is right: It is best to fail."

He no longer touched his books. Worrying about what he was doing, thinking about running away from the lethargy, came to him less and less often, and when it did, he would bury it in a new orgy, drinking with his two new friends.

*

On Christmas Eve, just before midnight, Andrijašević came out of the garden of the director's house and set off for town. The night was surprisingly quiet but cold. Stars shone brightly and vividly; snow creaked underfoot, and the *bura*—blowing until yesterday—had piled it up in some places into small hills.

The cold air immediately went to his head. Two days before Christmas Eve, he had mentioned to Minka and Darinka how sad the holidays are for people with no home or family. Yesterday he received a written invitation from the director of the factory to spend Christmas Eve with them. Jagan and Milošević were angry at this, but Andrijašević went, regardless.

It was cheerful and welcoming at the director's house. Although there were no children in the household, they decorated a Christmas tree. Respecting the director's wishes, they observed old customs on days like this, lit candles and sang a Christmas carol. The director's two nephews kept rhythm in unison with Minka; the older guests—among them Đuro—did the singing. Gifts were then exchanged; the director had bought something for everyone, from his wife to the maid. Because of some of the humorous gifts (Đuro was given a red flag and a trumpet as a 'revolutionary'), a humorous mood took over, especially with the director's brother, an influential merchant who visited for the holidays. Memories of prior Christmas Eves and stories of family events came next. Everyone was in high spirits—but Đuro was not happy. He felt like an outsider among them; they were talking about famous people, about relatives—the party was just for that particular family and not for him, a stranger. And in addition, he thought of Vera and her Christmas Eve.

"I'm sure she's thinking of me right now ... this will be desolate and difficult for her."

The director did his best to cajole him and offered him more wine.

Đuro did not protest, but the more he drank, the more lonely and bitter he felt. Unable to keep this up, he said at last that he had promised to meet his friends around midnight, thanked his host for his hospitality, and left.

Outside, after the first step, he felt he had drunk too much. In the warmth of the room this hadn't bothered him, but the freezing night befuddled him. He knew he could barely walk straight, and this sent him into an even greater funk.

"The only reason I went was to impose on them.— What do they know about my sorrows! They were having a fine time; they have the right. And I sat next to their enjoyment like a traveler who has no idea where fate will take him tomorrow."

Snow blanketed the town and was still falling steadily and evenly. The silence of the night and the magnificent sight of whiteness did not inspire his awe but, instead, disturbed Andrijašević.

"It's snowing ... Before the snow started to fall, carts clattered along the roads, and one could hear the pounding of footsteps. And now, even if a whole army were coming, you wouldn't hear them marching. The snow is falling on everything, stilling it all and making it all equally white... And meanwhile I, too, was slowly falling... It is burying me... soon it will cover me altogether... "

And again, Vera came before his eyes—dear, strong with all her intelligence and sophistication.

"I wish I could find Jagan and Milošević. Midnight... They'll be home."

But the house was deserted and dark.

"They must have gone to midnight Mass."

Đuro went looking for them. People were congregating, a few at a time, in the streets and hurrying to church. The church was already full; only the shadows of people could be seen in the almost total darkness.

"They are coming out of habit, not because of religious sentiment. And they are drunk—like me ... But still—these people know that they will be glad they were at midnight Mass and will get something from it that is good and beautiful. I am the only one among them all who is led by nothing here; not piety or joy ... "

He could not remain in the church for long. Walking down the street, he met a multitude of people who were just coming out from another church where Mass had already finished. The world was rejoicing, singing, gamboling about in the snow. The girls' voices mingled with the drunken singing of the older folk.

"This poor man who has been miserable for a whole year got drunk for the glory of Christmas Eve, and this cheered him up. He shouts, he sings; he is happy. They say that the wretched are worthy of mercy. Ah, what is misery compared to this wrenching pain of the soul I live with... "

Hoping to find friends, he went to the inn. But there was not a living soul there either. Tired and shivering from the cold, he sat at a table in the corner. No one came to ask him what he wanted. The waitress was chatting at the kitchen door. She didn't even turn on all the lights; the inn was half dark.

"Alone—alone—everyone else has somewhere to go; I have no home or relatives ... And I will never have any. A desolate, empty life ... ah, if only it could end ..."

After midnight, the place started filling up a bit. People came from their houses to end their festivities in style. Lukačevski was among the first to enter.

Andrijašević muttered a greeting.

"You don't seem to be in much of a mood. I'm not entirely well myself; I overate at dinner, so I am sure I won't be able to sleep. I was invited by the headmaster," (he was Lukačevski's newest companion). Lukačevski immediately started listing the foods he'd eaten and praising the headmaster's acumen.

Đuro couldn't listen. Every word—even if it meant nothing—cut through his brain.

"Ah, if only he'd budge from me! If only Jagan would come so we can escape somewhere! This one will do me in with his storytelling."

"But you aren't drinking anything! Oh no, on this very day! Here, I want to treat you to a drink for once. Micika, give me a bottle of Asti."

"Thank you, I don't want a drink."

"Come now, as far as I know, you are no softy."

"Good God, he is torturing me. What can I say to make him leave, to leave me alone?"

"Here, the wine is already here." Lukačevski poured slowly and spoke, obviously relishing the fact that he could drink cheap champagne.

"Thank you; I told you I will not drink."

"Now I warrant you won't offend me. To make this easier for you, let's toast to Miss Minka's health."

Ðuro touched his lips to the glass.

"I see it truly doesn't suit your taste. So sorry. Undoubtedly you drank better stuff elsewhere?"

"No."

"Were you not invited to dinner today?"

"Yes—but why do you care?"

"Nothing, nothing, I don't even know who invited you. It's not, of course, difficult to guess. You were at the director's. Nice. Nice."

"And why would it be nice? This is, I think, quite simple."

"Simple?" Lukačevski laughs. "Yes, so it is. You are often their guest."

Andrijašević wouldn't answer. It seemed to him that Lukačevski was deliberately asking stupid questions to upset him.

"Nice, nice. I'll be glad if this ends well."

"If what ends well?"

Ðuro felt his rage rise. "If he doesn't leave, I'll offend him. No, I will leave, myself," he thought and looked for how to slip out as fast as possible. But the inn was quite full of people; everybody was shouting, a few sang and spilled glasses and people were crowding in through the front door.

"He will see to it that you marry," Lukačevski said in his usual calm tone.

"What did you say?"

"He will see to it that you marry," Lukačevski repeated more loudly. Ðuro felt a sharply mocking tone and the intention to torment him.

"Please don't speak to me that way. I will not allow it!" he said directly in Lukačevski's face.

Lukačevski looked at him and laughed.

"So what's the fuss, my God! An everyday matter. You will do like a hundred others. They invite you into their home, then they will have you married off."

Andrijašević looked at the close-shaven, laughing face before him; the laughter seemed to convey ridicule for his weaknesses, his failures, and all he had experienced and suffered.

"You are stupid—you understand—stupid and rude!"

"What's wrong with you?" Lukačevski backed a little away from Ðuro, half standing and staring menacingly at him. "Please don't forget where we are. You are howling like a drunkard."

"You are a blackguard—a scoundrel—an evil coward." Ðuro spewed out a whole volley of insults. Even before Lukačevski could defend himself, he stood up and slapped the man with all his strength across the face.

Commotion ensued, a few rose from their chairs, and in flew the waiter and the proprietor. Lukačevski stood as pale as death in a corner and could barely speak to those who held him back from jumping on Đuro:

"Drunken animal!"

Andrijašević, when he slapped Lukačevski, was overcome by a dizzy spell. He wanted to lunge forward, raise his fists—a nearby lamp shone before his eyes like a vast light—he staggered and fell.

Chapter X

On Christmas day, he woke up late. At first, he didn't remember a thing; only later did all the memories of the night before begin to pass before his eyes. Christmas Eve at the director's, midnight, the empty inn, Lukačevski with his wine, his sudden fit of rage, mindless, his senseless urge to harm the man, to drive him away, the clash with him, fainting ... all the details returned little by little before him. He knew how they helped him up, rubbed him down with a towel (he had fallen hard and hit the corner of a table), took him home ... And he remembered Jagan, how he sat, drunk, by the bed, but not comforting him, instead fighting back his own tears.

"This is all embarrassing, nasty, contemptible... I could not resist hitting him... I'm completely helpless, my nerves aren't obeying me... Ah, and now, what?"

He didn't even want to think about it. He was disturbed by everything that reminded him that this affair would have consequences, he would have to get up, go outside, feel ashamed when facing people, and run away from them ... He could not stand the light of the day that broke through the window (outside it was sunny and tranquil). He crawled under the covers, closed his eyes, and wanted to lull himself back to sleep in the warmth. The wound on his head stung a lot; his whole body felt broken, pain stabbed him in the temples, and he tasted something dry and disgusting in his mouth.

That's how Jagan found him.

"Get up, brother; it's already two o'clock. Are you ill?"

"Leave me here in bed. I feel like never getting up again."

"What are you saying? Does your head hurt?"

Jagan carefully examined the place where Đuro had been injured the night before.

"It's nothing, it will pass. But you would seem to have a moral hangover. Admittedly, the whole thing is a bit ludicrous. And I was sentimental yesterday; you know I almost wept when they took you home? I must have been very drunk. Oh unhappy saints! The despair of loneliness and anger. Milošević and I were already *in cymbalis bene sonantibus* before dinner... And you know, when I think about it, you did the right thing by hitting the louse. He must have angered you with his sage advice."

"He was rude; he told me that the director wanted to marry me off to his daughter."

"And that made you angry? Anyway—a slap is a slap. No one can erase it for him. But you know, that's not the way to do it. He will lodge a complaint about you with the authorities, and the headmaster will conduct an investigation. If we let them work—we will not be able to laugh at their expense. Is it—you don't care about your job?"

"I don't want to think about anything today."

"Well, it's easy to think; he will drive you away as he did me. Till the end of the summer, there are no exams; and then the Pakrac decree will await you—you'll lose your job, my brother. You know what? We're going to scare them!"

"?"

"Lukačevski is a reserve officer. You say he insulted you, and indeed he did; Milošević and I will go to him and challenge him to a duel. Quite officially. This will scare him and he will undertake nothing against you. Instead he will sign a statement that he is to blame."

"Do what you want, I don't care. Just don't force me to get up and go out."

"Stay in bed. You'll get rid of the headache before dinner. I'm going to fetch Milošević. I should wear a black coat, but I don't have one. No, it's better if I wear an ordinary suit; one might laugh when they heard that we went dressed to the nines. Bye for now!—and wake up. And you should know, you smacked him smartly; half an hour later, he was still red on his right cheek."

*

Ðuro stayed in bed all day and the next morning. Jagan and Milošević visited him and reported that Lukačevski had accepted the challenge; he was not surprised and only asked for a 24-hour delay until he could find seconds.

Jagan rubbed his hands with glee. He was in his element. The eternal student in his soul had woken and relished doing something just to exasperate the towns-folk. He didn't think for a second that this duel might have disagreeable consequences for him or anyone else. He felt no concern about the future; he was aware that this would not end well, but he was thrilled that the present was so turbulent and exciting.

On the second day of Christmas, in the afternoon, Đuro received an official notification from the headmaster summoning him the same day. Đuro got up out of bed and set off, ignoring Jagan's advice; he wanted to ignore everybody and act irrespective of anyone else.

"If you go, you will end up quarreling with the headmaster, and then I will have to challenge him to a duel as well," Jagan ended with levity.

So, at the stated hour, Đuro knocked on the door of the headmaster's office.

He immediately noticed a change: the headmaster had moved his desk to the side, and another round table from the teachers' lounge, covered with a green cloth, was placed in the middle of the room. He sat at the head of the table, with Gračar and Maričić to his right and left; They gave Lukačevski a seat a little further away.

"What is this? A trial?" thought Andrijašević. Everyone greeted him without a word.

"Please sit down; we were waiting for you!"

The chair for Đuro was directly opposite Lukačevski's. He looked over at him and saw that he was as calm as ever. Lukačevski stared ahead, his hands in his coat pockets, leaning back a little. Andrijašević had to look at him if he wanted to look around the room, so he settled at an angle, facing Gračar and stared out the window at the muddy yellow facade of the opposite house.

"I assembled these gentlemen here today for an occasion of grave moment," began the headmaster, fingering a file. "To preclude any possible suspicion or error on my part, I took the liberty of inviting Mr. Gračar and Mr. Maričić. Let them witness this very serious and important conversation I will have with the other gentlemen."

The headmaster stopped. Everyone shifted in their seats, the chairs creaked.

"I must say, gentlemen, that the case before us exceeds my comprehension and expectations. What happened cannot be found in the annals of any institution for the education of secondary school youth. There are certainly no such examples in the history of the institutions I have served, including this one which has been entrusted to my care and supervision."

The headmaster stopped again and pretended to look for something in his file.

"To my great regret, I learned that on the night of the 24th to the 25th of this month at the Pod Nehajem Inn, an affair occurred that was inconceivable to the townsfolk and to myself, and certainly not foreseen by the authorities when they appointed these two gentlemen to be educators of the children of this country. I will not question the reasons or seek a culprit; that could steer me away from the intended path and dictate that I should follow rigorous official procedures and mercilessly remove—yes, remove—from the healthy body of this our institution the ulcers that have begun to appear."

Đuro noticed a wet stain on the opposite façade and began to focus with interest on the difference in color between the spot and the rest of the wall.

"I hereby note the fact that, to the dismay of all present and later the rest of the town, two gentlemen—Senior Teacher Lukačevski and Junior Instructor Andrijašević—were in said inn on said night after midnight, certainly not in a sober state..."

Lukačevski interjected: "Please..."

"Later you will have the right to speak. I hereby note that you exchanged words at that inn in front of a very mixed audience. On that occasion, Junior Instructor Andrijašević forgot to show respect for a youth educator and older friend and punched him in the face."

Another pause.

"To fill the cup to the brim, so that this is be full-blown disgrace, instead of a partial one, so that word about it can spread even further, after this appalling scene Junior Instructor Andrijašević behaved as if his chivalric honor had been impugned..."

Andrijašević shifted in his seat and looked sharply at the headmaster, whose voice immediately dropped to a lower note:

"...and demanded satisfaction from Senior Teacher Lukačevski."

"Why," Andrijašević continued in his mind, "did he immediately go to report to the headmaster? Was it that he was scared?"

"The gentleman to whom Senior Teacher Lukačevski turned to ask to serve as his second after he'd accepted the challenge—misunderstanding the duties of a teacher—was myself. It would be my duty not to say a word about this and instead to submit a report to the authorities, leaving them to decide how to proceed in the face of this kind of moral decay, which is all the more significant as it happened in a small town where every teacher must watch his step with extra caution. I did not do so, for the punishment from them would strike both who caused this sad affair, and I hold that you are not equally guilty. I can say without hesitation that Senior Teacher Lukačevski has never given cause for complaints, let alone scandals."

"Yeah, and now he's going to suggest that I ask him for forgiveness," Ðuro said to himself.

"I maintain that I am acting in accordance with my duty and conscience and I am sure of the approval of all of my colleagues and the entire faculty when I desire and demand that this damage be rectified if possible, to stop any further momentum, any further offense to the town and our youth—and to avoid being forced to pursue a strict disciplinary inquiry. I am seeking a way for Junior Instructor Andrijašević to ask his colleague to forget the insult and the scandal he has caused."

A long pause. The headmaster expected Ðuro to say something, but Ðuro just stared gloomily out the window, watching the early winter evening descend outside.

Gračar wanted to get involved, thinking of advising Ðuro to reconcile, but Lukačevski interrupted him.

"I do not want Dr. Andrijašević to ask for my forgiveness."

"Well, well, how magnanimous," Ðuro glanced over at him. Lukačevski's eyes spoke with cold contempt.

"I will assume, and so I must, that Dr. Andrijašević was caught up in a state of agitation, which I failed to understand, and my very presence aggravated him. I said nothing that could have offended him."

"Well, well, he's washing his hands and says I was drunk. Let him. Just for this to be over."

Andrijašević was starting to feel cold though the tile stove in the room was blazing. The agitation of the previous night had made him utterly vulnerable; he was suffering from fatigue and a longing for peace.

"It is good of you to come to the rescue of the entire faculty and me," said the headmaster to Lukačevski. "I believe Dr. Andrijašević," (he no longer referred to Đuro as junior instructor) "will forthwith behave equally loyally and fulfill our wish: to reconcile and let the regrettable event be forgotten."

"Tell them you agree," Gračar leaned toward Đuro, seeing that he was still scarcely present, staring out the window.

"I agree," repeated Đuro in a low voice, almost mechanically, after Gračar.

The room was nearly dark.

The headmaster stood up.

"The gentlemen will, of course, be required to document with an external sign that the affair on the night between the 24th and the 25th of this month arose due to a misunderstanding that has since been resolved. We would be best advised to go outside and stroll around the square at least twice, to put a stop to all the talk."

Everyone stood and grabbed their hats. The headmaster, quite happy that he had solved the affair his way (he was afraid it would affect his future career: there is no way forward for a headmaster of a gymnasium where teachers are fighting!), he donned his coat and, talking to Gračar, started closing the drawers. Đuro remained by the window while Lukačevski spoke in a low voice with Maričić. They left, the headmaster in the middle, Lukačevski on one side, Đuro on the other, and Gračar and Maričić on their respective sides. Neither Lukačevski nor Đuro spoke a word; the headmaster had to speak to the other two through them. They walked three times across the square, arousing a considerable sensation—people stopped and began to pay attention to this news. No one knew what to think now about the upsetting rumors about the duel.

Đuro walked mechanically, turned at the end of the square, and he returned greetings to passers-by. There was not a single thought in his head. During the third round, he said he had to go home, said goodbye and left.

He was freezing cold; a dullness and apathy sat on his soul. "As if it could end like that. I hated him at that moment—I hit him—and now this reconciliation! Apparently, I can't even be as crazy as I want—they won't even let me go to hell."

He was wracked by fever afterward for a whole week. By the time he got up, the racket had somewhat subsided; only in *Nova misao* did an anonymous note appear (Jagan had claimed that by judging from its sloppy style, it was from the retired teacher) in which there was mention of people who should be leaders, supporters of free-minded movements, who "de facto" act as "animals" engaging in thuggery and duels.

*

Đuro's illness weakened him quite a bit. He became even more irritable; he could barely continue teaching. When he entered the classroom for the first time after the illness, he noticed that the students were looking at him knowingly while whispering about him. He noticed the same thing out on the street: everyone looked at him as if they knew something and—so it appeared to him—provocatively. He greeted Lukačevski just as Lukačevski greeted him, never looking each other in the eyes; the other colleagues had never talked to him much anyway, but now they did so even less than before. Đuro was afraid they pitied him or believed him mad; because even Gračar and Rajčić demurred before him. So he ceased leaving the house; only when it was dark would he sneak off to Milošević's, returning to his apartment, tipsy, late at night.

One evening, Darinka met him on the way to Milošević's apartment. Đuro, restless and suspicious, immediately thought this was no coincidence—that she just happened to pass by at very moment.

"Ah, it's you, Doctor! Thank God I met you. What's keeping you in hiding?"

"I'm not well."

"Ah, because of that thing with Lukačevski? Fear not, Minka and I know what really happened. You know, someone else has also been feverish because of it."

"?"

"Minka. Poor thing. You must come to comfort her. She was terribly upset for you. She told me to thank you."

"What for, if you please?"

"Don't be so modest. She knows you hit Lukačevski because he mentioned her in front of you. She is grateful to you for that."

"That is not what happened."

"Again you are being disingenuous. But, dear doctor, why? Even if the matter ended a little coarsely, Minka still believes in you as much as before."

"What big words are you using? 'She believes in you!'" Đuro repeated almost angrily.

"Well, let's put it another way: she hoped and knew you would defend her honor."

"For God's sake, don't mock me!" Andrijašević was nearly shouting. Again he was possessed by the same hatred for everything he felt right before he'd struck Lukačevski.

"Oh, dear doctor, what's wrong with you? I do hope you don't think I'm insulting you when I talk about your feelings..."

"What feelings? What do you want anyway? Why were you waiting for me here, to interrogate me? To have a word with me?..."

"At this point, I must be frank because otherwise you won't understand, so here it is: Minka wept dreadfully and quarreled with her family at home over you. She said she would take no one but you, even if everything people say about you is true."

"What do you mean—take?" Đuro was drenched in warm sweat, and his hands were starting to shake.

"I mean that all this hasn't changed anything. She loves you as much as before and is convinced that you are worthy of her love."

Đuro cringed a little as if preparing for a blow to the head with a blunt object. He could barely walk alongside Darinka.

She recounted further how the factory director was angry at him, how the director's wife said she would not invite him over again; how Minka fell to her knees in front of her mother and wept, then was feverish for two days and finally confided everything to Darinka and begged her to talk with him.

"God, God, this terrible, awful! Wherever I go, I bring misfortune upon myself and others!"

Completely forgetting that Darinka was next to him, Andrijašević thought aloud about her words.

"What love! What faith! I never thought of Minka— she is as alien to me as any other girl! And I made her sad too!"

Darinka took his hand. They stopped.

"Doctor, are you still feverish? You don't know what you're saying. You pursued her, conversed and joked with my poor girl, and made her fall in love with you. We all knew that everyone expected you would soon become the director's son-in-law. It cannot be that you are oblivious to this!"

"Have mercy on me, not another word! Nothing, nothing, I didn't know—I was mad—and I am mad, just leave me alone—to rot without doing harm to anyone!"

"Then I must tell you that I, too, was deceived by you. Poor Minka! You are not acting like a real man."

Andrijašević could not listen. Although it was night, he left Darinka in the middle of the road and hurried to Milošević.

"No, no, time to get away. What further misfortune might I bring upon the people around me: Poor child... Can this really be so? Doom, ruin, as soon as possible— drown yourself in alcohol, disgrace yourself, so that no one can see you anymore, you must flee from everyone so you can die like an animal, unknown and with no one to grieve for you."

That night he couldn't stomach two glasses of wine. And his heart was pounding fast and hard as if he had been running a long time uphill. He lay on Milošević's bed, unable to muster the strength to go home. Jagan stayed with him for a while until Đuro dozed off. Then he shone a light over Đuro's face and said quietly to Milošević, as if afraid of his own words:

"This one will be going into the darkness before us all. On his face it's written that he will die young."

*

In Zagreb, January 14, 190*

Dear Sir!

Having established with you a year and a half ago some parameters under which you were allowed to count on my daughter Vera's obligation to you and vice versa; to fulfill that obligation to her, I thought you would devote all your efforts to the goal you allegedly had. That is why I did not want to believe the rumors that reached us from Senj, still hoping that by taking care of your exam, you would justify my trust and my wife's. Now, however, I hear that you have not devoted even an hour to prove yourself worthy of our daughter's hand and that you are also keeping dubious company. The crowning of all your deeds was a duel done over a girl in your current residence. You will realize that after these facts, you cannot expect any further considerations from either our daughter or ourselves since this matter was reported to us by an utterly reliable person and was the subject of a report to the authorities, as I have since confirmed. Although, in my opinion, this is also redundant, I return to you at my daughter's express desire your letters and ask you on her behalf to do the same with all the mementos you possess of hers. Please consider your obligation resolved.

With regards

Ivan Hrabar

./. Shipment enclosed.

Đuro read slowly, without surprise, word for word.

"And that, too, had to end ... of course ... Everything, everything will fall, disappear: one thing after the other."

He waved his hand as if pushing away a part of the past. His gaze fell on the package on which Hrabar wrote the address in his own hand.

"Look, a beautiful part of my life is written in that package ... And now I no longer live the bitter and sad life anymore; a time of even, sure despair has come. Preparation for the end. Yes, we will finish."

"I cannot dare to be alone."

He remembered that while he was ill, after the affair with Lukačevski, he often stared at a fixture on the ceiling where a large lamp had earlier hung, and which now remained naked, ominous.

And he cast down the letter and went to Jagan. He slept after lunch.

"Get up, let's have a drink. I need something strong."

"Ah, you're sentimental again. Agreed—just where to go? Milošević has no more wine; elsewhere, they do not serve on credit. We owe too much. Wait, wait—ha, a man always remembers when he thinks: let's go to Frane."

Frane was an innkeeper on the outskirts of town, on a sunny hill, overlooking the sea.

"It's winter, so you can't sit outside; there is no space inside, but Frane can be swayed to extend us credit."

· · ·

Late that evening, stunned, barely able to stand, Andrijašević came out of the small, smoky room. Outside was a quiet, holy night. The sea murmured calmly, splashing into tiny ripples in the bay.

"Are you whispering? Calling me? Are you? No fear, you don't have long to wait. I'll come, I'll come."

As if speaking to a living creature, he raised his head to the sea; from the tranquil noises he clearly heard the summons of the end, the last act.

Chapter XI

"All of life, the whole wide world, is merely a dream, a beautiful dream ..." sang Jagan hoarsely, holding his glass high.

He and Đuro were the only guests at the Italian tavern, who had started serving wine three weeks before at an old warehouse by the seashore. During the day people stopped in at the Italian's, including folks who measured coffins for a living, wheeler dealers, and others who were seeing to business along the coast. There never were guests at night; the Italian's tavern was not outfitted for a better clientele. In the evening, the low-ceilinged, dark room was only dimly lit. Half of the space was occupied by barrels; a mirror in the corner and two paintings from Radetzky's military campaigns were the sole furnishings. The Italian was a new innkeeper and hoped to attract guests, so he gladly sold on credit. This is why, as Jagan said, he and Đuro set up camp at this 'inn.'

"Pepa, bring us another!"

A disheveled girl with devilish eyes and half-bared breasts brought another liter.

"Where are you running off to? Sit with us for a while!"

Pepa immediately obeyed and sat on Andrijašević's lap. The Italian was not strict with his servants, and the 'thin doctor' appealed to a girl who, before becoming a 'waitress' at the Italian's, washed dishes and served at the worst dives on the narrow streets of the town.

"Drink, Pepa! That's the only thing, after all, that still makes any sense!"

"Drink and kiss, huh?" Pepa laughed loudly and pressed her leg along Đuro's.

"Lovemaking is no good. It is not worthwhile," philosophized Jagan. "Wine is better than women; you taste it, and if you don't like it, you spit it out; but a woman will sit on your back. Wine is beauty and intoxication—the third liter reveals Muhammad's paradise. There is freedom in wine because it binds you to nothing. And love—to hell!—it makes the heart and head ache. Only Pepa and women like her can be loved; they ask for nothing but time."

"That's right, long live Pepa!"

The girl kissed Andrijašević loudly.

"Doctor, my dove, you'll get drunk again. Don't pour so much into yourself."

"Let him at least do this, ma'am," Jagan shot back. "We don't ask for anything else, do we, eh Đukan?"

"Just look at yourself in the mirror! Your eyes lit up like a cat's," teased Pepa.

"I'm beautiful! A man who is honest to himself," boasted Jagan, self-mocking, gazing at himself in the mirror. "And the two of you are so beautiful in the mirror that it's as if someone painted you. There is something Shakespearean about this hole in the wall."

Pepa turned to the mirror, and with her Andrijašević. He couldn't bear his reflection for long. His eyes stared at him, expressionless, from the mirror; his red, swollen face, surrounded by a disheveled, untidy, long-unshaven beard, had the appearance of a seriously ill man.

"Ah, we used to be prettier," Jagan returned to the table. "Ðuka, do you remember when we changed our shirt cuffs every day?"

"Drink, don't philosophize—you'll make me angry."

"And yes, you were still doing that last summer. And for three years, I have been pretending not to know I was supposed to change my shirt weekly. That Englishman had the right idea and killed himself because he found undressing and dressing so boring. And what's your shirt like, Pepa?"

"Fingers to yourself, you rogue!" The girl slapped him lightly on the hand. "It's just for my doctor," and she leaned closer to Ðuro.

He sighed.

"You are indeed all I have left. Let's drink!"

"'Let's get drunk with wine, love, beauty,'" Jagan began to recite Baudelaire's verses.

The Italian called Pepa from the kitchen.

"It has been over half an hour that no one has sought the floor; I do so now, and I beg the glorious company to listen to me." Jagan raised his glass. "I drink to the health of the most beautiful of all doctors and his one true love, our fairy queen, Pepa! Cheers!"

Ðuro downed his drink to the last drop.

"Leave love alone—why is that on the tip of your tongue today."

"Ah, am I offending your memories? Forgive me. I, too, am sentimental; I am affected by Milošević's illness. He spits blood as if he were being paid for it. You see, he'll be the first to go. Then it's our turn. 'Like two beautiful mid-May flowers'—ha ha! What about Minka? You're no longer visiting her family?"

"I am not!"

"Well, say something, for God's sake; I have to keep up the banter the whole time. What's got into you?" Andrijašević took an envelope from his pocket.

"Go ahead, read."

"*Vera Hrabar—Tito Ljubojević—to be married.* Who is this?"

"My fiancée."

"Well done, that's beautiful. And when is the wedding?"

"Don't torture me."

"It would be nice if it were today. I would hold a speech in their honor, and at the end, for a lark, we would announce your engagement to Pepa. A woman is always to blame. A crazy Kraut put this nicely: *Er ist ein Dichter stets und hängt am Weibe.* But that doesn't apply to the Kraut. He drinks beer and makes babies. We Slavs are slain by women; we cling to them like ivy to a tree trunk. Hey, Pepa! Come, lest the knight weep..."

Clutching each other by the arm so as not to stumble, Jagan and Đuro dragged themselves out of the Italian's tavern. They were nearly unconscious; they only had enough strength to button up their coats and stagger forward. The April night was warm, dry. The rain that had been falling over recent days had stopped; the streets were drying up in the southerly wind. There was a powerful southerly blowing wind from the sea—somewhere from a vast distance waves were coming, the water level was higher than an ordinary tide, higher than the shoreline, flooding the coastal road. It was as if the sea were furious, out to swallow up the houses within reach; the sea rushed in and swept away the dust and rubbish from the roadway. The air was laden with a heavy, unpleasant odor.

"Darn, it is pouring as if it means to swallow us!" Jagan hugged his friend.

They passed the pier in the middle of the harbor. Along the pier, there were sloping, paved recesses onto which boats could be pulled out as needed. The rocky shore here couldn't break the wave; it spilled over a long stretch and formed a giant muddy puddle.

Andrijašević stopped and stared at the wave that had almost reached his feet.

"What are you waiting for?" asked Jagan.

"See how it beckons!" muttered Đuro darkly.

He could not clearly express what he had in mind; his tongue was tied, while there lived only a presentiment in his brain of something difficult that he, nevertheless, must do.

"You could go into the sea very slowly today," he said in a whisper, took a step, and found himself on the slippery face of the slope.

"Stop; where are you going!"

But Đuro wouldn't let himself be stopped. Jagan, staggering, tried to grab him by the coat, but the wave drenched them up to the neck and swept their feet along.

"Help!" Jagan shouted suddenly, feeling solid ground give way beneath him.

Two finance guards and sea pilots ran in and, with effort, dragged them onto dry land.

Andrijašević seemed to be in a fog, neither feeling the wet nor hearing Jagan's curses.

Jagan was instantly sober.

"Now, that was an accomplishment! Where are we going to go, all wet like this? Any minute the day will dawn. If daylight catches us, we will make a fine parade. In town, the kids will be laughing at us tomorrow. We're not going into town. Let's go off somewhere."

Djuro followed him without thinking. They boarded a steamer about to leave for Rijeka and took it to the first stop.

*

"You could not reproach me for my treatment of you," said the headmaster to Đuro, standing and staring at him. "I closed first one eye, then both of them, using your young age and poetic nature as your excuse."

"Talk, talk if you like—who cares what you're blabbering on about," thought Đuro, who stared blankly ahead.

"But this last thing is neither excusable nor forgivable." In a drunken state—of course, with a colleague who unfortunately belongs to our institute, but, I hope, not for long—in a drunken state, you nearly drowned the day before yesterday. You weren't at school yesterday—you offered no apology; in fact, you weren't in town!"

"Talk! Talk as much as you like—none of this is making sense."

"Have you no shame? Shame before the citizens, the youth who have easily learned of your exploits? You came here two years ago; I had high hopes for you...," the headmaster started listing warnings and advice.

"Ah, what's the point of listening to him! It would be wisest to walk away and leave him. It doesn't matter because either today or tomorrow he will fire us anyway, as Jagan says."

"You were an intelligent young man, educated, calm, well put together ..."

"This is his eulogy for me, yet here I stand before him, still alive."

".. in short, I am now compelled to act with due severity: I am issuing you an official reprimand to be reported to the competent authorities."

"Just let me go! Don't torture me—issue the reprimands but do not pulverize my nerves!!"

"I do hope you will take this reprimand seriously and consider its consequences. Although I am forced to resort to such strict means, one of the last, remember, I am counting on you to improve."

"If he doesn't stop, I'll run off. I cannot listen to him—I'll lose my composure."

"We are all concerned about your progress. Why aren't you studying for the exam? The deadline is near; you know the condition the authorities imposed for you when it appointed you as a junior instructor. Get rid of that friend of yours who lures you and is the worst possible company; all of us will all be on hand to help you advance in your vocation and help you move ahead..."

Andrijašević felt rage and the urge to smash something. His eyes filled with blood and tears.

"You, you will help! This is all your fault; you have killed me, destroyed me, you and others like you!" he shouted, raising his shaking fist, almost in tears. His pained, inflamed eyes hurt the headmaster; he remembered the fight with Lukačevski and took a step back.

Andrijašević noticed the fear registering on the headmaster's countenance. Vast contempt and compassion at once filled his whole being.

Tears streamed down his face; his whole body trembled.

"Don't be afraid, no—I won't hurt you. I'll get out of your way myself—I'll go—I'll run away on my own," he said slowly. And barely staggered over to the garden.

*

The heat that summer was horrific. The sun did not allow people to work or move about. Bathing and walking in the late evening were the only remedy for the stultifying heat.

With all this, Andrijašević did not leave his room during the day. He was ashamed and afraid of people. He remembered how everyone had begun turning away from him; Gračar avoided talking with him, resentful that he was being constantly called upon to teach Đuro's classes. Toward the end of the year, Đuro didn't even go to school every day; the binges with Jagan often ended at dawn, and occasionally outside of town, where the two of them fled so they would not have to stagger back at the break of day, searching for their accommodations. He reported being sick and secretly spent evenings at the Italian's.

At home, he was beset by creditors. His former landlady, to whom he owed two months' rent, came looking for him every week. He was used to her cursing him from the stairs in front of the servants. No one gave anything on credit anymore; his shoes were torn, and stained threads hung from the hems of his trousers. His underwear was in tatters, and some of his clothes were confiscated by his former landlady; he didn't even think about wearing a suit.

The Italian stopped running the tab when he discovered Jagan had been fired. Since one must eat, Đuro found a tavern under his apartment, patronized by a lower–class clientele. There he sat in the evening with whoever came along, the town clerks, caretakers, and sods, for whom no one knew how they subsisted.

Towards the end of the school year, Jagan went to some relatives to pursue another occupation. Both were sad to part ways. After that, Andrijašević was left alone—so alone that he felt as if he'd been imprisoned in a dungeon and the only way out for him was—the gallows.

He seldom thought of Vera, very seldom. Sometimes it would occur to him how much she must have suffered because of him before she gave herself to another man—but his belief in destiny, which had reached him intact and for which he was not to blame, did not allow him to repent and mourn his lost life.

Intoxication became a physical need. He ate barely enough for a child, but at night he could not sleep when he came home sober. On these evenings he would be haunted by terrible thoughts; he could flee from others, but not from himself. This is why he kept himself inebriated over the holidays after the school year ended and lived in an unending state of wooziness.

There were times when he stayed at the tavern all night and the next day till lunch. He did not dare go home because he was afraid he would be unable to fall asleep from distress and agitation (his nerves were already shot and his hands were thin and shaky). He drank wine in the afternoon, returning home late at night. But the alcohol was often insufficient for him to overcome his nervous tension; Đuro would go to bed and try in vain to fall asleep. Every rustle hurt him as if someone had stabbed him in the brain; he had the feeling, at times, that someone else was with him in the room.

The lamp had to burn all night. He took a book and used all his strength to concentrate on the letters. But the words made no sense, and whenever he turned the page, he would shudder, thinking someone's face was on the new page. He was fully cognizant that this was a hallucination, but to no avail. Images arose from the corners of the room: people alive and crystal clear, who would only move when he closed his eyes, but then they'd immediately come crawling out from the other wall, at the foot of the bed, in the window recess. This battle with hallucinations sometimes went on for hours and hours; he was half-aware of what they were and knew he would go mad if he believed in the reality of these phantoms. This frightened him, and on such nights he loudly declared to himself that this was but an apparition—he should not give in to his sick brain—but the faces of people he knew, even literary personalities, marched so vividly before him, and he struggled with their commanding, mocking gaze.

One night he thought he saw Milošević talking to him at the foot of his bed, half-dead, with bloody patches on his cheek. He clearly heard the man's wheezing, sickly voice. At this point he was abandoned by the last shred of consciousness he had fought to hold on to, thinking that once it was gone, madness would come for him—and he began crying out for help. His landlady was scared to death when she found him half-naked, in rags (he hadn't had even one decent shirt for such a long time), crouching by his bed, kneeling on the floor and, staring madly at the lamp, he was flailing his arms against something invisible ...

He remained in bed for two days after that night. On the third day, he felt worse; he could not endure life without wine; and though he could scarcely stand on his two feet, off he went to the tavern.

He lived this way for a month, fearing he would go mad and drowning his fear in his daily mindless drunkenness. At the end of the holiday, he received an official notification from the gymnasium administration that the imperial regional authorities had fired him as a junior instructor at the Senj gymnasium, as he had not satisfied the regulations regarding the qualifying exam for a permanent position, pursuant to the order of the day, d. m. y.

Chapter XII

Toša!

I address you as neither beloved nor dear; such titles seem silly in this letter, the last I will write.

Yes, the last. My life has aggrieved the people around me and disturbed them. My death will make you grieve.

But this is how it must be. Time to bring this to an end—to find peace—forever –

I could tell you my story—describe my life. I haven't the strength—my memories are fading—and I am in agony.

I'll tell you only this, so you know of my end: I have been utterly ruined without salvation. I have quarreled with everyone, fled from them all, and feel ashamed. They tortured me like Christ; they drank my blood.

I drank to avoid thinking; I became a miscreant to escape from life. And then Vera married –

But why write all this to you? Listen to this last piece: Two weeks ago, I was fired. I was left alone, helpless, in a fog. I sat in a tavern and knew that they allowed me to eat and drink out of pity; because I had no hope of ever paying. I waited. I drank and waited. The end. Death.

They are right. Yesterday they kicked me out of there. They didn't let me drink. Why let me disturb others?

So I left. All I took with me were several sheets of paper, my diary—these notes. You will see what I wrote first at your place in Zdenci and later in Senj.

I don't know why I'm sending this to you. Maybe to further deceive myself about how I used to be better, so my death won't seem as terrible as it truly is.

I escaped from Senj. I went on foot, by road, at night, in the rain. The sea beckoned to me, but I did not obey it right away; death is not easy.

Now I see—the time has come to die. I found my way here today; I don't know what the time was. I found a corner at this tavern where I'm writing to you. They look at me strangely. But I was starving and my stomach burned. I still have silver buttons on my cuffs; I will pay with them. Ah, and if they throw me out—so what, why should a man care who is going to his death?

But I must drink—I need strength to die. So the phantoms don't pursue me. I'm shaking—will you be able to read this?

My life was vile, sad. And who is to blame?

I have thought about this—and I haven't solved the riddle. Was it my upbringing, that they fashioned me into a poet and a writer and imposed upon me demands that life could not match? Was it my love for Vera that could not end well because of the misery and penury of my position? Are the people around me—this little town, vicious and petty? Was it the alcohol, the reveries, feeble nerves, or a disease of the soul?

I don't know, I don't know. I'm silent: time to end. Time to escape to the end—to flee from this vile, shameful life.

You see: it seems to me that I have always been fleeing from people and life. I never put up resistance—I always stepped aside. And when I came into contact with the life people lead, a life in poverty and straitened circumstances, I fled from them too. I also fled from myself, not wanting to see myself fail, drinking instead, and waiting for the end.

I am going now. It is night—and no one will see me outside. Like a criminal, I also have one last wish before I die: to smoke a cigarette—but I'm ashamed to ask for fear that they would bring me the bill at once. I'll toss them the buttons and skip out.

I hear the sea murmuring. It is beckoning to me; it's late.

Goodbye, Toša! Be cheerful and happy. If you have a son, don't tell him about me.

Đuro

(At the bottom of the letter, the letters were scraggly, blotched, obviously by tears. Toša came to Novi three days later to bury his friend. But Đuro's corpse was nowhere to be found; maybe the *bura* had swept him over to the other side.)

In Trieste, late January 1909